THE PEACOCK AGENDA

Marko Vignjević

MONTAG

First Montag Press E-Book and Paperback Original Edition August 2018

Montag Press
ISBN: 978-1-940233-57-4
Jacket and book design © 2018 Niall Gray
Managing Director & Editor – Charlie Franco

A Montag Press Book
www.montagpress.com
Montag Press
1066 47th Ave. Unit #9
Oakland CA 94601 USA

Montag Press, the burning book with the hatchet cover, the skewed word mark and the portrayal of the long-suffering fireman mascot are trademarks of Montag Press.

Printed & Digitally Originated in the United States of America
10 9 8 7 6 5 4 3 2 1

1.

An Evening On the Water

On the night of telling, Ayda Ayduk drove from the morgue to the river in his car. There he got into his motor boat and sailed to beneath the bridge where he waited. As always, during such nights, he wore binoculars around his neck, a somber but hungry look about his face, his eyes bearing the wait of the steps he was going to take.

Manipulating the engine and the rudder he would occasionally take a look, quite a look out at the bridge, through his binoculars, and when seeing a woman mount the railing of the bridge he motored toward her. He saw, and this in an enlarged perspective through his binoculars, as the woman straddled the railing and then seemingly seamlessly stepped sideways onto the bridge's outer space, though with a look about her depicting no fear, at least none which was visible to Ayda. Prompted by that move of hers, he rushed into a faster traversing of the water, the woman holding on to the railing now behind her back, her arms positioned as if in an image of a relenting crucifix. She looked tired.

Not wanting to draw attention to himself, let alone make her self-conscious, Ayda Ayduk turned off the engine of his motor boat, drifting toward the ever nearing bridge. No longer needing binoculars to see her, which at the time now hung round his neck much like the woman's dive he had anticipated. There, Ayda let out a murmur, utterly below the strength of his voice -*Beautiful eyes, beautifully dive*- and thus, as if in a must, the woman's railing of choice parted from her hands, ever remaining with her arms loosely limp out of joint and limb, especially those joints, those of her shoulders...she looked as if she was being born anew.

Still in his motor boat, still amazed at the sight of the woman's dive, an opportunity was presented to Ayda Ayduk to reestablish the working of the propeller. Having done so, he reapplied his hand to the rudder of the thing, unable to peel his eyes away from the unfortunate flightless, yet moving through the air, creature. She wasn't tumbling or rolling, there was no spiral to her and what is more, and of this Ayda made a memory mark, she let out no sound, gave no voice. Though in awe of the scene, Ayda Ayduk felt uneasy, not because of her demise, but rather because he didn't get to hear her voice. And as he was traversing that small expanse of the river remaining until the bridge, he imagined it, he imagined it was soft but clear, resonant but mild in tone, unambiguous of timbre and yet soothing to hear, seeing how he had not heard it. Thinking about the lack of compensation for interest shown, Ayda did rejoin the scene, it was precisely at the time the woman was about to hit the water, and when that time came in earnest, Ayda Ayduk crested over a wave, quite the river wave, utterly tiny, barely perceptible, but he did feel his motor boat rising along it and dropping slightly in its wake which made him raise his eyes at the exact aforementioned moment when the woman lowered herself, and upon the water of waves past, their eyes met and she too smiled at him.

She kept that smile on her lips when she hit the water, after which Ayda, now with the look of a loved man on his face, heard a loud snap, wondering whether it was the churning of the river in the place of her fall, or the whipping lash of her neck braking due to the impact of flesh on liquid.

Having neared the place of the tragedy, Ayda again turned off the engine of his motor boat which was being struck anew with waves, only now they were waves caused by the adding of the whole of the woman's body to the mass and sum of the river. Ayduk quickly set to his reason for being there in the first place, and under the brim of his motor boat he got out a hook fastened to a long steel handle that can reach far and deep. And reach it did, guided by Ayda's expert hands holding on to it, running it right beneath the surface of the woman's watery grave.

No bubbles?! he mumbled. A notion of her having died upon impact as he rushed his hands along the hook. The conduit sounded the contact with the body through his upper extremities giving him enough sense to derive a thought from the feeling under the water of placing the hook under her slowly sinking body. That having been done thus, Ayda began the work of dragging the body out of its still life.

The first thing he saw, the thing that belonged solely to the woman, was oddly enough a blown up bubble of her bubble gum. It had floated out her first, not having burst in her dive into the water. So perplexed and petrified was he by that image, of her diving, chewing the gum as she arced through the air, that he nearly let her be, but it was made clear moments on that in fact the bubble and all the gum she had chewed before it was formed was just stuck in her hair. It's just that he noticed it first, that's all.

Now present in the moment, Ayduk pulled her to the gunwale, grabbed her under her arms, where in all her body felt like water in a spasm, it being cold, and, granted, parted with her soul, but regardless. Ayda went about loading her into his motor boat with a manner similar to which morticians would load a coffin, or as he imagined. It was then that he, without loitering or stalling due to the fact that he could still see that final smile of hers on her lips, stood up, swayed toward her, and standing over her turned her face down in his motor boat. There, Ayda Ayduk settled at his imagined command post from which the better part of his vessel's labor was generated, from which he motored back to the shore.

Well within reach of the river bank, Ayduk turned off the engine. Though he saw no one on an eventual evening walk along the summer strand, he was urged to a caution by a sense that what he was doing was wrong. That being how it was, in silence which resounded only through the smacking of the water against the body of his motor boat adrift, Ayda Ayduk reached down to the starboard side grabbing a body bag he had stowed there and brought with him from work.

It wasn't easy for him, putting the body into the bag, you see. The water remained stubborn in its liquid state of aggregation, the motor boat rocking, you understand. To top it all off, a dewy kind of mist was falling down making the black plastic of the thing slippery as was the weight of the body of the woman. Not troubled by what needed to be done, also not wanting to begin the usual practice of his routine, Ayda did manage to bag her. Doing so, of course, first with the heavier portion of her corpse, followed by the depositing of her two legs, and her arms and head.

Leaving her in a state of complete plastic attire, and having felt the shallows of the river mounting into the beginning of land beneath the hull of his boat, he proceeded, in a further intent of disembarking, to reach for an ore lying wrestled beneath his feet. Now in his hands, motioning with it through the wet, to the river bank upon which he then landed.

Once firmly on land, as heavy set fellow as he was, Ayduk had no trouble hoisting the bagged body onto his shoulder, and with an intended gait, striding toward his car, parked not far from whence he had left for the water. But he was a nervous type, proof of which was the fact of him relinquishing the body to the ground, taking those few steps back to his motor boat, and hailing the vessel out of the water completely, worried that it would get dragged back and further away down into the river. It was then that he, with the boat secure, not knowing why, took a breather, nothing much, you understand, just a transient couple of minutes to breath. Now, during those couple of minutes, for the first time that evening everything felt right, a feeling which quickly prompted him to retrace his steps, which he did with haste, back to the bag of a womanly shape, the forms delineated on its plastic black surface.

The long bag zipper up the front of the bag shimmered in his eyes, the plastic sides hiding his undertaking from anyone who might have passed by, as he suspected they would at any moment. Shouldering the body up again, Ayduk was presented with his first real challenge. There were street lamps along the strand, and though faced with this aspect regularly in each of his evening outings, that night they seemed particularly ominous to him. Lifting the heavy bag, he bobbed and weaved through the lamps, dodging the cones of light that fell on the roadway on his way to his car. He made no pauses; there were no deviating movement on his part aside from his zig zagging from the artificial lights beams.

Occasionally acquiring a firmer grip on the plastic of bagged corpse he would prop himself with the bend of a knee in a brisk, swift motion, which made the body he was carrying resettle on his shoulder in a firmer and more solid position. And in doing so he neared the trunk of his car, which had never been that far off.

With the load still on his back, Ayda took out his car keys from his pant pocket. They shined just like the way in which the zipper of the body bag shined. He impregnated the trunk lock with a metal turn, produced from his wrist, after which, upon hearing an unfortunate, though unavoidable creaking of the hinges the trunk rested on, there came about a sudden break in the process.

"Ah, dinner!" a man said, having approached Ayduk.

For lack of will to turn his body, Ayduk's eyes turned instead, themselves capturing within their circumference a metal badge designating the man's affiliation with the city's police authorities.

"Ohm, I suppose..." Ayda replied confused.

"Don't like eating alone, do you, sir?"

Dreading such an ending to his venture, Ayduk felt the weight of the body on his shoulder for the first time since disembarking. What is more, he thought he did not have the option to put the body down into the maw of the trunk, now gaping open as was his mouth. A crank needed to be pulled, and there was painfully pressure lacking on the lever of his habituation in such a reality. Generally, Ayda Ayduk didn't bear stressful situations like this all that well.

"No matter, sir, you needn't trouble yourself. So a man gets hungry. So what? You know..., I saw it."

"You saw it, officer?"

"When she made her climb over the railing, looking down. When you lowered your binoculars, looking up. When she hit the water and sank. When you started your engine again and dragged her out onto your boat. I saw it all."

"Well..."

"Do you trade in the stuff?"

"No, this is for me. I was just hungry. You see, it's dinner time, like you said."

"Oh, for own purposes then? A citizen, carry on then!"

With that, the police officer turned on his heels. Ayda's gaze, still transfixed on their talk, met with his sight, the back of him going away further along his beat. Ayduk loaded the trunk of his car, locked it and got behind the wheel setting the motor into action, leaving the motorboat nestled on the strand.

As the car began to move so did his thoughts. He'd heard of such happenings before, such specific behavior on the part of the authorities, and though he knew that it was common practice, such dietary habits of his fellow citizens, he was never able to accept them personally, to practice that kind of gormandizing out in the open. He was also unclear on the point put forth by the officer, namely that of trade, or any trade in the stuff.

Too hungry to think further, with the job of preparing the meal ahead, Ayda Ayduk let his car drive his trouble away. He knew only one thing for sure: many a life is wished away thus. Therefore he ceased with his questions and the prompting cues for possible answers, his grip became relaxed, his eyelids limber, his forehead smooth, his trunk thumping in the twists and turns of road along which he came home.

2.
Dinner Time

On a metal slab in the freezer adjacent to the kitchen, Ayda Ayduk busied himself with the body he brought home. He made sure to close the door, as was common practice with all rooms in which cold was produced.

One could hear those sounds coming from the freezer unique to the preparation of meat. One cold almost imagine what he was doing. The rest of his apartment was quiet. The lamps on the various stands gave no light, the AC was turned off, the blinds on the windows were drawn half way, the kitchen table wasn't so much set as it contained a frying pan, a bottle of sunflower oil, a pot with the appended vegetables resting by it. There was salt and pepper on the counter top, a jug of red wine breathing with its opening clear. There was a calendar hanging on a wall which parted the two panes of the kitchen windows, and a day framed in red plastic hanging over it.

But a hacking sound did get out from inside the freezer. Ayda was dismantling the cartilage bits of her corpse; afterwards a kind of silence was instilled in which a slithering sound of him tearing her skeletal muscles off her bones was presented to the freezer's outside, devoid of anyone who would be bothered by what he was doing. Then came the noise of a butcher's knife scratching the surface of the metal on which the corpse lay, being how it had already made its cut through the spindle shaped smooth muscle tissue.

What did he do with all that blood? No shushing, smacking was heard. Did he drain it from the body? Could he be storing it somewhere in his freezer? A kind of soup, perhaps.

Regardless, along the time-span of his work, Ayda Ayduk got to thinking about the specific cut he wanted for dinner. Stalling on the epidermis of her integument, and having looked the corpse over lengthwise and crosswise, he decided to have her ribs for his meal.

During the whole time, no one came bothering, not once did his phone ring, while in the living room chair a thumping hacking of his hatchet dwelled only upon the darkened screen of the TV set.

Aside from the freezer, the place was dormant. A newspaper was lying on the coffee table, disabled from spreading the news by a snooze, be it even by means of an overly ambitious paper route through the flat. The wrinkled spines of books lined the shelves of one particular wall, particular in the way it was uneven in relation to the other three walls. They were mainly text books on pathology and anatomy and such. He did like to take his work home with him.

After the sound of Ayda depositing the remainder of the disemboweled carcass into various spaces of storage in the freezer had hit the chair placed at the head of the kitchen table, he emerged from the freezer in a billow of vapor ice and particles in all cold. Imbued with such a heat of low temperature, and passing by the said table with ribs in his hand, Ayduk moved that chair, claiming his place of dining.

He put her ribs directly on the table and poured the sunflower oil into the frying pan. The stove was made ready in the turn of a dial, a turn which came none too soon as there were quiet grumbling sounds being emitted by his stomach. While the pan was heating up, Ayduk seasoned the meat with plucked rosemary spikes, rubbing them along the former parts of the corpse's axial skeleton. Upon hearing the sizzling on the pan he raised his eyebrows knowingly, and lit from on high by a bulb of light, allowing him to see better. Then Ayduk gave rest to the ribs by putting them in order into the sizzle of the sun flower oil.

While he did this, there was a woman's hair resting around his elbow and a bother about the front door of his apartment. The brisk knock was repeated, but it shouldn't have been, because during its fourth performance Ayda was already there with handle in hand.

"Mister Ayduk?" a young man said at the door.

"Krot, what is it?"

"Mister Ayduk, you forgot... Oh, you're having dinner, I'm interrupting..." he said as he heard the sound, smelled the smell and saw the sight of a set kitchen table in the background.

"Forgot what?"

"Right, here you go, sir."

Krot handed him an envelope and attempted a quick departure from Ayda's door, but Ayduk, though sound of hunger, was still present of mind and he opened the thing examining its contents right then and there.

"Wait, wait. Let's see what you brought, Krot."

They were papers, findings he had made earlier at work. None too pleased with that development, Ayda slightly extended the arm which held the papers, as if making Krot sniff them.

"Who said so?" Ayduk asked.

"The chief did... Oh, you're having meat for dinner! I was just about to myself..."

"The chief told you to bring this to me?"

"Yes, sir."

Reluctantly, Ayda accepted what he had received from the young man, who he now perceived wanted to come in, ever slightly inching the tips of his shoes toward the threshold of his apartment with a wetness on his lower lip.

"Is there anything else?" Ayduk asked.

"Yes. You're expected tomorrow."

"Tomorrow? Sunday, tomorrow?"

The young man's toes stopped advancing toward the door, in all he seemed to have realized the audacity of his transgression.

"Yes. It's all in those papers."

"Thank you, Krot. Goodbye then."

"Goodbye, sir."

Leaving by way of elevator, having liberated the view from the window of the stairs' landing, Krot was finally gone, enabling Ayda to approach the window, and the bare bulb overhead, holding both findings and the envelope in his hand. Looking out, he remained transfixed in a restful scene of the street below where a woman, all by herself, was just walking by. She was having a snack which had been served to her in something like a paper bag but different. The bag had a grease stain on its bottom, and was held by her hand of long bone-expressed fingers. She had no other bag with her, no purse, and no satchel, which seemed strange to Ayda. Without inquiring about her choice of snack, Ayduk saw her taking, one by one, a piece of food and gorging on them fiercely, the deep fried fingers, nails and all.

A cringe penetrated his toes which were forced to stretch and strain inside his slippers, but he continued to watch the woman, hoping that their eyes wouldn't meet, and that she won't smile at him if they did. Having had enough of her snack, the woman in passing, let her hand and the grease bag in it rest by her side.

Ayda heard the elevator bell sounding and the elevator door opening on the floor below. The beat of heels of a man's shoes harmonized alternating in a climb, prompting Ayda to head back to close his apartment the door which he had left wide open.

"Good evening, neighbor!" an elderly man panted, finishing his ascent.

"Hello, mister Balaban."

"Working at home I see," the neighbor said, seeing the papers in Ayda's hand and the remaining ribs on his kitchen table behind him.

"Excuse me?"

"Your dinner, Ayda. Your dinner will burn. Can't you smell it?"

Ayduk rushed into his apartment unintentionally slamming the door behind him, adorning the old man's lips with a portending smile. Balaban then walked a pace or two, taking his keys to the lock of his own, letting out a shout for Ayda through the door and further speaking softer:

"You and your meat!... Poor, poor man."

Inside alone, the kitchen table was set in earnest, a fine plate, knife and fork placed where they should be. On the stove the ribs turned for the last time, letting the fat and juices presented in a human form not long ago melt into the pan. Ayda Ayduk filled his plate at the stove, relenting from his hold over the plate only once it was placed between the knife and the fork on the wooden surface. He extended his arm wanting to manipulate the chair into a more suitable position for sitting and eating, when, nervous as he was, he declined his own intention upon remembering that he had left the apartment door unlocked.

In going about fulfilling the last order of his tick, Ayda made sure to look through the peep hole through which he saw nothing that could've explained his state of mild anxiety toward all things and the people belonging to the outside. Hoping away from the uneasiness of someone knowing he was feeding on human meat gave him a point of retreat which led back to the kitchen table. Despite the fact of it being the norm and with certain citizens even a matter of pride; it was something he could never admit to, seeing how he too was human as well.

Sitting down for his dinner, Ayduk failed to notice that string of woman's hair still wrapped around his elbow. He aided the food prepared, aided it on its way to his innermost, hollow-most part with a glass of red wine. He didn't find that the drink had breathed out all of its qualities much praised at feeding time, so he didn't hold back from sipping and swallowing in gulps.

He had his meat and wine, had his vegetables too, and was about to start clearing the table and ridding the dishes of tracks and traces of his gorge, when the door of his apartment again became bothered and he with it at the twice repeated knocking.

"Sorry to bother you, Ayda. The damn post man mixed up our mail again." The neighbor Balaban was seen there voicing his complaint.

"Can you see that here?" and Ayduk was handed a bill in an envelope.

"Do you have mine?" he continued.

"I haven't checked my mail box today."

"Would you mind?"

Ayda looked at him.

"Don't look at me that way. I'm tired, I'm old, and I grow cold easily. Besides, I've watched the news and it's off to bed for me after this."

As Ayda gathered a cluster of keys from the hall stand, he examined them, as if looking for his mail box key, when in fact he was just playing with Balaban who was extremely patience deficient. The way downstairs was headed up by the old man who apparently had an aversion to everything which made things, tasks, chores and alike easier, including the use of the elevator.

"On the way back we're taking the elevator," Ayda Ayduk gathered aloud.

"Let's compromise," Balaban responded. "We'll take the elevator together, but we'll get off one floor below ours and walk up the rest of the way."

Luckily for Balaban, Ayda was walking behind him, leaving the old man outside of the realization of the expression on his neighbor's face depicting outer recognition of self in Balaban who got to the mail box wall on the ground floor first, executed a turn-about face and waited for Ayduk to open his mail box.

"There is something in it. Hold on." Ayda said as he jammed the key in again.

"I'll give the postman something to jam about the next time I see him," Balaban foamed away.

With a move of pulling up and out and pulling away, Ayda Ayduk opened the metal door to his mailbox and exhibited a post card addressed to the old man. Admittedly wrinkled and apparently caught in the very door of the mail box and not deposited through the designated, what is more, designed crack of an opening, Ayda apologized and handed the sole post card to his neighbor.

"Thanks, Ayda. This is all I have left," the old man said.

Then Balaban turned around stepping toward the elevator door, out of which a young woman was exiting at the time. Walking past them, she left their building not having bothered, neither herself, nor the two of them with any greeting. The old man held on to the elevator door tapping his fingers on its outer side as if running them over the keys of a piano in scales.

"Common, you hungry man, we'll take your cursed elevator all the way up to our floor."

The mail box door was shut, letting the ground floor air through its tiny aluminum gills, atop of which stood his name in full – AYDA AYDUK – and he himself was in the elevator, doors closing, going up.

Toned down by means of his enzymes' labor, Ayduk un-wound the string holding up the blinds in his bed room. Listening to them falling down and meeting the foot of his window, he was interned into a state of sleepiness which he didn't want to give up.

The weather was warm, it was the summer's end and it was an end that was being prolonged through high and higher air humidity, barring the subjective feeling of temperature, meaning

Ayda had no need of dressing for bed, no desire for further clothes, be they as light as virgin's hair. Debating the matter of whether to tend to the dirty dishes now or not, having in mind that he will be going to work tomorrow, Ayduk brought all the misgivings, and with them all of his inborn nervousness to an end. This end or, if you will, the beginning of his state of rest, manifested itself with a lolled walk into the kitchen, the turning off the lights in the rest of the apartment, and while he was going about it, why not, the repeated checking and making sure the front door was locked.

He ended that day upon a pillow of white cotton. He positioned himself on his side, leaving the arm closest to the mattress with no pose but the one in which it rested, bent in the elbow with his palm as a pedestal for his cheek. As he was drifting asleep, he did indulge in one last motion; it was a motion of his tongue. He licked his lips and in doing so he felt that woman's hair still around his elbow. He took the feminine follicle between the thumb and the index finger of his other hand, extended his arm holding the string way outside of his bed, made a move with his fingers as if he was salting a soup to taste, giving the follicle a release, and remained lying, into his sleep.

3.
Live Free and Die Healthy

"Krot, Krot! Where is that kid?!" The chief medical examiner Zokora yelled upon the opening hours of the morgue.

"Ayda, have you seen Krot, and if not, have you any idea why he isn't here?" Chief Zokora restated his quandary directly.

"No I haven't, Chief. Plus we're out of coffee," Ayduk said stalking the coffee pot, barren as it was on the counter in their office.

Chief Zokora paced the room, the floor lined with Veronese green linoleum. Occasionally sliding and squeaking along its surface, he wouldn't raise his eyes, not wanting to put Ayda into a rushed state of mind due to him possibly perceiving it as his responsibility, the absence of Krot, that is.

"It's eight of clock! No coffee, you say? Could we scrape something together, do you think?"

"No, Chief, there's nothing left to scrape. Look ..." Ayduk took the coffee pot into his hand, raised the hand holding the thing and fingered its bellied glass surface along the scales designated in a print of the color orange.

The Chief walked, and he did so without grimacing, to and fro between the walls. At one point he yielded at the cabinets hanging on the wall. Prompted to a browsing, a search had begun for a fresh, unopened can of coffee. That search manifested itself with an abundant ambition of the Chief's hands, which questioned not the look of the scene they had brought about. But Ayduk saw it. Aside from the fact that Zokora was an old man, he saw his boss's youth bursting forth in a death of an extinguishing tumor of amber. Through the words the Chief was saying, Ayda clearly imagined a younger, stronger Zokora, and a Zokora who had had coffee whenever he wanted it. Ayduk wasn't made to feel unwanted in such a beginning of a working Sunday, on the other hand he wasn't made to feel prompted to act, not regarding the whereabouts of Krot, nor regarding the coffee state of their office.

"There's nothing here! So it's true: nothing will give us rise today!" Zokora proclaimed.

"I could try and get coffee, Chief." Ayda offered.

With that, Zokora was put into a kind of stillness, but as he was, feeling like a father to all who worked under him, the Chief refrained from any confirmation of his colleague's suggestion, speaking while holding his hand in a shape it would have if it had contained a coffee mug in it:

"I hear something!"

Zokora went to meet the sound he heard, doing so with brisk steps, surprisingly brisk, seeing how he was devoid of the dark drop beverage. While this was going on, Ayduk remained sitting in a lounging pose, laid out, with his back putting an inordinate amount of pressure on the chair caused by the relaxed condition he was in. He was looking at his shoe laces.

"Sorry I'm late, sir," Krot spoke to the Chief as he entered the room.

"It's eight fifteen of clock. Where in rigor mortis were you?" Zokora had no exclamation in his sentences.

"My girlfriend barely let me go this morning."

"You fucked last night?" the Chief was still waiting for the young man to come to work.

"Tore it up I did."

"Kid, in every man's life a realization sets in, mostly too late, that it's quite the other way around." Zokora wanted to put the subject to bed.

"The other way around, Chief?" Krot felt like a kid again, not understanding.

"Yes. He realizes that it was he who got fucked."

"But, Chief, she did things to me."

"What things?"

"Well…, down there," Krot looked at his crotch where his answer was rooted.

"To a kid like you, an ideal blow job, is like pissing in the wind," the Chief, it seemed, really was beginning to need his morning coffee.

"But… I have no other excuse for being late, Chief."

"Good. If it's hard and straight, it's healthy." Zokora put his hand on the kid's shoulder and informed him of the worst. "We need coffee, Krot. Coffee is what we need."

"I'll go to the store, Chief. I'm on my way," and he was.

Calmed by the resolution of the issue, yet put into an expectative state, Zokora neared the table, buttressing himself with his fists on the surface of the thing, and looking much like an ape as he gave off a smile which remained idling far too long in the stuffy light of the morgue. Seeing his boss relieved of mind and relaxed of limb, Ayda Ayduk got up, in his place the warm began to radiate from the seat of the chair he was formerly in as he made his way to a small window installed up high on the wall.

Met with a view that couldn't endure due to the height of the pane, Ayda propped himself on his toes, leaving his hands restful in his pants pockets. Behind him he heard another chair, not his former one, being dragged along the linoleum floor to the extent sufficient enough for an older man like Zokora to have a seat, and when Ayduk turned briefly around he made sure that it was so.

There was a morning paper on the table. There were the Chief's hands grabbing the leaves, and a whole world he never wanted to know stood to attention for him to behold and perhaps care for. Not commenting on the edition, giving not so much as a sigh which would make a more inexperienced coworker join the goings on of his soul, Zokora rested his back as Ayduk had done earlier, continuing to sift through and stray away from the urge to have his morning coffee.

"He'll be here soon, Chief. Don't worry." Ayda aided his boss. "Thanks."

As if called forth like a libation-substance-bearing-cherub by what was said, Krot penetrated the metal-barrier framed door posts. They flew apart, the doors did, and through them the kid stepped almost ceremoniously, for that was how he held the can of coffee he had purchased, aloft, up on high. Krot acceded to the table speaking something as if appeasing a god. Then he had the can of coffee torn, ripped away from his fingers, as the Chief loaded the coffee maker once he did away with the coffee's product attire.

There was also something else the kid carried in. Ayda took it when he got the answer as to its nature, use and purpose. A caring though confused young man, Krot had bought breakfast too. While the coffee was on its way they did away with the newspaper, clearing the table, getting out the cardboard plates, plastic cutlery and what not…, well, not much else actually. The kid took out chubby pieces of meat fried in a heavy kind of batter. There were also condiments on the side, and three packets of factory-made pudding. All three of the men sat down and began breakfasting.

"Aaah, nibbling on a cribling," Zokora said.

"You did well, Krot," Ayduk added.

As if on a mission, after a well-timed pause between a chewing and a swallowing, the kid pulled away from the table, leaving marks of pale on the linoleum made by his chair because of what he did. They looked like stretch marks, as he came to the coffee pot in a complete boil of brew. Krot got out the coffee mugs from the cabinet above. Knowing how everyone took their coffee, he neither asked nor commented by affirming what he was cognizant of. In this way, the gentlemen of the morgue were served, each according to their liking.

"You're not going to have coffee with us?" Zokora inquired with the kid.

"Thank you, Chief, I already had my morning coffee... You know."

"A defeatist! I like it," the Chief ended with a sip.

"You're not going to finish that shoulder blade, mister Ayduk?" Krot was gesturing around Ayda's paper plate.

"Help yourself, kid."

And with Ayda's finger's nudge, Krot's gesture was brought to a reaching which evolved into a grabbing which was then a grabbing no more when it was a biting off of meat from the shoulder blade on the part where the kid's teeth were set in.

"When's the meat guy coming?" Ayda inquired with the kid.

A good moment or two passed before an answer would be provided, for Krot was of a mouth full and of fingers dismantling the little but succulent meat there was remaining on the bone. Wishing to acknowledge the question, Krot raised his index finger having dispatched it from a repeating motion mentioned before. While doing so, and with his cheeks stuffed, looking like a horny old goat's prostate, the kid swallowed, licked his lips, swallowed once more as if to see the bite on its way, and answered wiping his hands with a napkin:

"He should come at around nine."

"Nine of clock?!" The Chief provided the gathered ones with a blast of sound.

"Yes, sir. That's the arrangement."

"Don't worry, Chief, the meat will keep," Ayda rested him assured.

"We can't have corpses piling up. Decomposition holds out on no man!" Zokora exclaimed.

In learning such a lesson, Ayda and Krot looked at each other, not at all staring, let alone expressing doubts about certain aspects of Zokora's well-being. They knew it was hot. They mutely concluded and agreed that it was the swelter of the summer dying that brought the Chief to such an irritable state.

"A refill, Chief?" Krot asked, already holding the pot in his hand.

"I suppose."

Ayduk followed the process of the refilling of Zokora's mug somewhat uneasily. There was no sense giving his nerves more tension and cause for agitation and other deviant thoughts and tendencies. But Ayda always was a nervous type. Only he saw a self he never admitted to in Zokora, especially a Zokora in an expectative state. Therefore Ayda goggled his eyes at Krot, well one eye to be precise, the eye farther away from the Chief. The kid's reaction to such a reprimand was made obvious to the errant party prompting Krot to immerse his upper lip under his lower one, elongating the region of his face below the nose in a stretched out but relaxed protraction, and softly, unknown to the Chief, shaking his head negatively.

There was heard a metallic ringing at the door of the morgue. The kid departed toward its source while the two seated men were finishing their coffee, Ayda as he always had, and Zokora, unlike before, very much in agreement with the unfolding of their working Sunday routine. The Chief had enough of Ayduk's ever present, ever repeating silence, and being bored with himself, waiting for the meat guy to come, he hoped that the prior ringing at the door was indeed in that regarding, and so he asked:

"Is it always like this with you?"

"I do get breaks occasionally."

"And how do you spend the time of those breaks?"

"Why do you ask, Chief?"

"Because I don't see it in you."

"See what, Chief?"

"The ever-present isolation."

Krot returned in no rush, informing the men with his greasy lips, shining in the news that the meat guy had indeed come. Remaining without an answer 'till further, Zokora was the first one to get up, followed by Ayda's rise from their chairs.

There were certain expanses of space between the three of them, but nothing so intangible that it couldn't have been bridged with words, and that span of phonemes linking up into lexemes was laid, traversing, in good time, by way of Zokora's order:

"Let's get to work, gentlemen. The sooner we end it, the sooner it'll begin."

And they did, the kid being the first one among them to do so, going through the office door again to meet the meat guy standing with his work order fastened to a hard pad in his hand. The Chief made his way next, but before going the way of Krot, he suddenly stopped in his tracks, making Ayda, who was following him, halt his muscle work. Turning round just with his upper body, quite in a by-the-way manner, whereupon the Chief said:

"Mark my words, solitude diminishes nothing, it only amplifies it."

4.

Calvaria

Walking home, passing by a completely glassed wall, Ayda Ayduk turned his head toward it and decided to go in.

He was charged for his entrance at the door, and having designated a proportional amount of money from his wallet, he deposited the sum charged with a slim young woman wishing him enjoyment and a good evening.

The art gallery was packed with people and talk, wall to vault. All things exhibited were crafted out of marble as white as hasn't been seen outside of the quarries of Carrara. Statues and statuettes, figures and figurines stood exposed, as Ayda learned, for the first time in their existence that night. There was no paint about the things aside from the colors reflected off the peoples' clothes, ironically so because of the radiating light off the white marble that created a shy but very real outflow of pigment.

"A glazed toe, sir?" a young man bearing a serving tray broke Ayduk's concentration, at the time focused on one magnificent piece.

"No, thanks."

Ayda decided to see the young man on his way, and in such a sight he noticed that as the cater waiter moved closer to the center of the space, winding along the binding crampedness of the gallery, his hors d'oeuvre offerings became the more declined by the attendant art lovers. This seemed strange to Ayduk because he saw nothing that would rally such a unanimous waving off of the service, nay, the food that the young man was providing to those in desire of it. Therefore, curious, he followed him, doing so with utmost caution for fear of his interest in the matter being brought to light. He wanted no such shine of any such light.

With eyes transfixed on the cater waiter's upper back, stopping when that one would stop and repeating the mentioned move, Ayda received clarification to his primary question. Enlightened on the point of the cater waiter facing constant rejection, he stood before the center piece of the exhibit.

Standing all life size, the sculpture was of two halves. One half was made into a man, an old man with his arms extended onto the horizontal, his head held high, and his eyes wide open and he had a thoroughly apathetic expression on his face. The other half was also made into a man, a much younger man, and that half was crafted with its back to the back of the older man. The expression on the young man's face was contrary to that of the old one's, and his eyes were closed. The young man also had his arms extended in the same horizontal, lining up and as if merging with the ones of the old man who was as if carrying him, dragging him along. There was however one detail made more than obvious, as was the entire piece itself. The young man had been crucified. Clearly visible on the inner wrists of his hands were two large nails. The spikes were put in place, one on each inner wrist, and were clearly visible penetrating the old man's inner wrists with their points protruding. It was a double crucifix.

Both men that were depicted had beards. The older, upright one had short, and the young, drooping one had long hair. To reiterate: the older man's head was held up high, the younger man's head, by way of its chin, was held by his collar bone.

The aspect of the sculpture with which the artist had struggled the most with, and this was obvious, were the feet of the young, crucified man. They were not crossed at the ankles. They were not dragging on their heels. One foot was presented as if in a propping motion, whereby it rested solely on its larger toes, leaving the heel of his foot to ascend with the heel of the other foot. In addition, the other foot had a bend in the ankle to it, an outward bend, with its sole exhibited toward the first foot. As far as the legs of the crucified one were concerned, the leg bearing the bent ankle was slightly angled at the knee, and in the hip. It too was making an outward move, while the leg of the foot propped on its large toes was presented firm and as if laboring, it was positioned straight from hip to nail.

The body of the older man was not much to talk about, a notion so obviously expressed by the sculptor through the old man's face. And though he was depicted as old, he did look as if he had yet a bit more to age still. While in the presenting of the young man the stone cutter made sure to emphasize the structure of him, in the old man the structure itself, the unavoidable aspect of every human form, was expressed through his skin. Whereas the young man seemed to derive the strength and power of his position through the strength and power of his bones, in the case of the old man it was the opposite, it was as if his skin was holding him upright.

The musculature of both men was depleted, probably because one was dead and the other was old. Somehow the stone holding the young man looked pale, almost the color of a young babe's skin. Contrasting it was the color of stone holding the old man, it was much rougher; one could almost see the many sun beams deployed on it over the years.

Oh, one more point of thought. Being a double crucifix as it was, there was no possible way for any of the audience to view it as a whole. It was completely split into halves, two aspects of two halves, as it were. If you were to look at it in a way in which you could get a view of both men together, you could do so only by looking at their sides, in profiles. If, on the other hand, you wanted to view each of them individually, you could do this only by looking at the enface of just one of them at a time. It could never be seen as a whole.

"One must pick a carcass apart, for what is death for?" one viewer said.

"A marvelous stone," another replied.

Ayduk circled the piece slowly because he wanted to get a better sense of what was going on with him; he also wanted to hear people's thoughts and comments on the piece. Never in the know, as far as art was concerned, he made sure to try and stop at as many possible view points of the sculpture, for it was surrounded by a thick belt of people, more knowledgeable than he, appropriately attired for the opening, meaning that he was a bit distracted by all their colors. He should've come during day light hours, but still.

"We don't see much religious works these days," a woman talked to her friend.

"It's impressive how an archaic motive, due to it not being used for a long time, once exhibited again becomes very much an original. Don't you agree?" the friend asked.

"You're right. The same as we would find a caveman walking among us original and unique, while in his own time he was probably boring to his friends."

"Regardless, I do like it."

"I know. It's so with all people."

Ayda didn't grasp the concept of admiring a human body, dead or alive. Perhaps it was because of his occupation, perhaps because of his lack of art appreciation, regardless he was stumped by their talk, and yet he could not tear himself away from their explanations, learning something else about himself that night, that he was an eaves dropper, an audible voyeur. So he hung around.

"It's such a pure stone, but in such a variety of color."

"Look! Look at his toe. Is that corn?!"

"A-ha, modern man!"

He made another move along the periphery of the sculpture. Of a lightened mood then prior to coming in, he remained standing behind two gentlemen, or in the least two men trying to pass themselves off as gentle, seeing how they were already men. Their dates were in front of them, and while the two women were admiring the thing, with the ever present reminders of *–No touching!-* by the staff of the gallery, the two of them were giving each other hint-full looks regarding each of their expectations as far as the further progression of the evening was concerned, hence the 'passing off' remark. "Will you be bidding?"

"Is that a possibility?"

"Yes. I know the gallery owner, he told me."

"Then I think I will."

Not being able to take any more of their "Oh, by the way." remarks and clues of that nature, Ayduk took it upon himself to detach himself from the thick belt of admirers of the piece. As he took his shoulder into a completely new and far direction, away from the flock, he was stopped by a conversation concerning the thing about which he himself began to wonder. Unfortunately, this made him reconsider his departure and he came to the conclusion that there was more to art than just works, there was the interested audience as well, provided you watched and listened to them in their irritated state. And so he heard:

"Such a brilliant artist."

"I know him."

"Really?"

"Mm-hm," a man gave sound infusing himself with champagne.

"Is he here?"

And with a champagne flute still in his hand, set on pointing out the stone cutter precisely with that hand, it being the hand that held the champagne, he clarified with the gesture of a museum curator about to seek retirement.

"There he is."

Where? Which one is he?

"The man in the leather jacket there."

"That one?"

"Yes, that one"

While the excited/agitated mixed duo expressed their opinion on the look of the artist with his work now passively behind their backs, Ayduk slowly made his way toward the group surrounding the stone cutter. Walking on and away from the ones which showed him the way, Ayda noticed a seemingly unseemly character who was becoming ever unbecoming of an artist, at least his notion of an artist. There was nothing about the look of him which could possibly, at any time, give away his occupation, let alone the criteria and standards' level at which he evidently practiced his art.

Just when he was getting near enough to catch an utterance or two of the man of the hour, his focused stride was broken by the very same man when that one stepped out of his circle of friends and in front of his audience with a champagne flute, the like of which had been provided to all present. Not wanting to feel out of place, Ayduk gestured mildly to a passing cater waiter taking a glass as well when the stone cutter raised his, speaking through a smile.

"Ladies and gentlemen, a toast, 'The longer we live, the guiltier we are!'"

All present raised their glasses, the majority concurred with what was said, and that being thus, they neared their flute's rims to their lips, perked for a sip, when a dissonant voice was heard from the backdrop.

"Go stroke yourself, you hypocrite!"

The sound came from a brusque looking fellow adorned with a frown under a head of unruly hair. He stood defiant in the face of a leisurely talent, the proprietor of which therefore felt called upon to raise his glass once more, being that his toast was interrupted, or at least the drinking portion of it, that being the most important portion. With his skillful arm extended toward the angry man, angered as much by that very gesture, the stone cutter's tongue motioned these words—

"My good man, a simple eye sees things simply."

And while the majority was going —*Here, here!*- the angry man turned in a confrontation with defeat, stomping for the exit, repeating, "Out of my way!" a phrase once ago quite dramatic, but in our present time utterly humorous in such circumstances.

Ayda himself left the gallery about thirty minutes or so later. No, he met no one more there.

5.
A Failing Death

Once more on the river. Again in his motor boat. As before frequently looking through his binoculars, placed over his eyes so as to capture the near side of the bridge.

With the day in a phase of transition to a darker blue, Ayda saw the man clearly. He was leaning on the railing of the structure. Ayduk was certain he knew the action of choice the man was going to take next.

He rushed the propeller's churn and the water was rushed by it. He looked down at the hook and the body bag, both made ready to accept his food of necessity. Once into the mid-course of the river, he noticed there were other vessels boating alongside his. There was a school of them, right parallel to him.

The night regatta was an awesome sight, and Ayda did make a point of admiring it for a while. But having done so in a matter of minutes during which he inadvertently slowed down the propeller's churn, he was set onto a thought that such an occasion could be to the detriment of his plan. Somehow such goings on were always going on without him.

Ever absent from the stream of others, Ayduk joined the night regatta, doing so, until farther, from a distance, by having a look at the people and their boats motoring opposite him, through the optic medium of his binoculars. He began to smile as he neared.

Ordered to a state of beauty, the vessels he was looking at were of a very fine appearance. Atop their masts the signal flags of a maritime affair were fluttering to the side of the wind's choice. Some were even giving off smoke through their cylinder smoke stacks crowned with a stripe of a color meant to contrast the remainder of the thing. Making bigger or smaller waves, depending on their tonnage, the vessels carried people on decks, visibly decided on the night regatta, and not failing in doing so. The people were holding things of food and drink in their hands, and occasionally, through his optical enabler, Ayda could see a hand here and there, occasioned, much like the vessels themselves, with ornamentation such as time pieces and diamonds in the rough no more, all the objects, their ordered boats included, were settling their resonant shine atop the transient yet eternal body of the river water below.

At one point, Ayda's eyes met with the eyes of a woman looking straight at him through a pair of binoculars of her own. The smile his lips bore not long ago became an image through her lens of a cramped pucker. The woman noticed him, hence she raised her arm discretely and waved to Ayduk who then sharply turned his head, along with his optical instrument, away from her and to the direction of the bridge and that man. Immediately he realized he shouldn't have done so, because he gathered as much that the woman looking at him would turn her gaze toward the bridge as well. That's exactly what happened, and Ayda saw it happen too. Playing an innocent, which he actually was, regardless of his misconceptions about what he considered taboo, he let loose his binoculars from his hands which then remained dangling on his neck, their weight hitting the arch of his rib cage, and began puttering with that hook and body bag beneath his feet. Realizing that the woman participating in the night regatta might see his tools, thereby reading his intent, and perhaps imparting the information she would have gathered to someone else, Ayduk was again brought to attention, realizing he shouldn't have done so, and stopped with the rummaging through the things he had in his motor boat. But he couldn't help it, briefly and ever so repeatedly he would turn to the woman on the deck of a boat across the way, and briefly and ever so repeatedly she would wave to him as she did when she found him. For no man is stronger than himself.

Further from the pillars of the bridge but nearer to the place of the man's perceived fall, Ayda turned off the propeller churn. The motor boat rested on the water's calm surface until he took the oar in his hands. Before the fourth stroke of the thing, not knowing why, perhaps because he was wishing for it, Ayduk raised his head, making sure the man was indeed on his way down, where the river expected him in the wave-less calm.

The man's feet broke the surface of the water first, and the rest of him moved it that much apart. Plagiarizing the river's appetite, and satisfied at least for that night, Ayda went about satisfying his. Nearing the place of contact, he had a careful look below, bending outside of his motor boat. With his hook in hand it began again. The dragging didn't last for long, not as long as Ayduk had anticipated. He hooked the waist of the man's pants and pulled him in closer. When he grabbed the suicide victim under his arm pits, in an approximation of his own as to the possibility of being spotted by that woman, Ayda loaded the man onto his motor boat not even bothering to have a look at him, and resting on his hook tip planted on the floor of the hull, he watched the night regatta from an upright stance, not noticing that the woman was still looking at him through her binoculars, having seen it all.

"What's created in kind is destroyed in kind." Ayduk said to no one.

A slurping, smacking sound was heard behind his back, and it remained echoing in a choke as it always will.

"What?!" the man was alive.

Ayda rushed his hand holding the pole of the hook; he rushed to lower the thing to its former resting place. Taking one step toward the man lying in a daze, spewing water from his throat and from his mouth which was further mute.

"Can you move your toes?" Ayda asked of him.

The man just coughed choking. He did so by covering his mouth with his hand. He shook his head, meaning he didn't understand the question, or at least its purpose.

"Could you wiggle your toes for me?" Ayda repeated.

It was funny, the man raised his eyes, as if wondering about the matter himself, he threw back his head, doing so slowly, getting a good upside down view of the bridge above, and he shook it affirmatively.

"Good. Then your spine remains intact. Rest easy now. It's Okay."

The man shook his head negatively, he coughed a few more times, doing so less violently with each cough, again covering his mouth with his hand, and said:

"I'm Pavle Pechuli, taxidermist."

"Ayda Ayduk. Good to meet you."

"Meet, the man says!"

They both smiled at this. Of the two of them Pechuli began laughing first and soon Ayda's laugh followed. Pavle got into a sitting position and had a look around as if he was in a new world. In doing so the scene of the night regatta didn't escape his eyes.

"There's a much better view of it from up there," Pechuli pointed to the bridge behind and above his back with a smile.

"I'll drive you home. We're going ashore."

Turning on the propeller churn again, being himself at the far end of the motor boat at the time, Ayda noticed something floating in the water. Not able to discern what the object was, he reached for it anyway; where he reached and grabbed a shoe.

"Is this your shoe?" he turned around holding a dripping piece of foot wear.

Pechuli looked at his feet noticing that one of them was bare, he motioned recognition of the truthfulness of Ayda's claim, all be it propositioned in the form of a question.

"Yes it is."

When the transaction was done with, Ayduk sat down making waves in his stead. He turned the boat around, and motored back to the river bank where his car was parked while Pechuli put on his one never sinking shoe. Not liking the feel of wet leather against wet socks, Pavle took off both his shoes just as soon as they found their place on his feet. He then took off his socks as well.

"I suppose death is meant to be uncomfortable," Pechuli said.

"You're lucky it's summer. A winter's death is ten times more uncomfortable." Ayda conversed.

"Better I never find out. And I'm certain you won't have the need to do so likewise."

Once on the mid-course of the river the two men perceived the scene of the night regatta across the way from their landing. The slender ships and the bulging boats illuminated the dark of the water, running on, and running down the sides of their hulls. A lull set in between them, which was indiscernible seeing how they had just met, and that calm absence of talking provided a notion which needed to be verbalized. The notion in question, or rather, that which caught Pechuli's eye, was one boat in the night regatta. Ayda knew which boat it was from when he was cruising toward the bridge. As before, the mentioned vessel carried that one woman, who then as before was still looking at Ayduk through her binoculars, having watched everything unfold.

"That woman is waving at us," Pechuli verbalized.

"All she does is wave," Ayda responded back.

"Give me you binoculars, please," the man asked.

Ayduk handed him the optical instrument. With his eyes and therefore his eyesight attired in an enlarged image of what was going on parallel to the two of them, Pechuli informed Ayda on what he saw with an occasional cough being expelled from his throat.

"She is, she is waving, at us," to which Pechuli extended his arm up high, gesturing a greeting with a metronome like motion.

Looking on at the night regatta and its most prominent participant as far as Pechuli was concerned, Ayda followed Pavle's example, only instead of having the woman in clear sight, he had only one question on his tongue:

"Why did you jump?"

The binoculars fell away from Pechuli's face, at least from the portion of it which served for looking, but which was then turned toward the man at the rudder as if still listening to the possible reverberations of the query. And as he had no illusions as to the fact that he, Pechuli, was the rescued party, Pavle felt called upon to put his rescuer's mind to rest.

"Didn't you want me not to jump?"

"I'm not sure."

"That's perfectly understandable."

"Is it?"

"Yes."

"To everyone?"

"Who else is there?"

Pechuli returned to viewing the night regatta.

"She's giving me a thumbs up," Pavle claimed, providing the woman with the same gesture.

The firmament was not being coy about its look, presenting it in fine, rarified shrapnel of stars above. Everything made everything more true. Besides, it did work, you know. Pechuli did put Ayda's mind to rest. Ayduk realized it once they were on the brink of the bank. It was then that a friendship had been installed.

"I'm glad I met you, Pavle," he said.

They both dragged the motor boat aground, Pechuli barefoot. He carried his socks and shoes in his one hand letting the other one rest in a deserved pendulum swinging by his side. Ayduk walked next to him, leading the way to the car parked under a very giving street lamp. At the passenger car door, Pechuli looked back to the place where the night regatta still abided. From that distance it was almost made into a memory. Modeled after his better judgment he said nothing, although he must've been cold, but rather he waited for Ayduk to take the lead as concerned to their departure from the river. And it was so, his belief that Ayduk wasn't a hopeless case, not yet any way, was reaffirmed when he heard Ayda telling him to get in the car, doing so through an order which even a lesser man would obey. They started toward the junction at which a pause was instilled in a manner tangible only to the car's neutral gear. Once the ride began again, and they were driving to Pechuli's apartment, for Ayda wanted to make sure all was well with the man, and so a brief conversation was brought to be, initiated by the driver of the thing.

"You said you're a taxidermist?"

"Yes, that's right."

"What kind of business is taxidermy nowadays?"

"An infrequent one."

Subtle smiles were brought to slight chuckles which rose into a short lived roar of the two men making their way to Pechuli's home. Not being able to recall the neighborhood he was driving through, and in general this particular part of the city, Ayda didn't hide his ignorance, for the times were precious to him.

"Am I going the right way?"

"Just keep driving straight. We'll be coming up on a turn. I'll let you know when."

In time Ayda did make that turn, after which came the curb of the sidewalk in front of Pechuli's building. There Pavle gave him his business card, wet though not smeared, and got out of the car. During the process, Pavle invited his rescuer to visit his store, he also propositioned forth a point of dining with which Ayda concurred, and then Ayduk made him remain stationary with another question:

"What are you going to do now?"

"I'm going to take a shower. I have river reek all over me."

"You are not going to try and jump again?"

"No I have dinner plans."

The passenger car door closed in a mutual recognition of their humor, manifested through Ayda's laughter as he was pulling away from the curb, and Pechuli's smile as he was climbing the steps to his door. Ayduk drove back home hungry. But there was meat waiting for him in the freezer.

6.
The Peacock

The chime of the bell was prompted into short repetitions, disturbing the airways in a dangle swinging above the front door of the taxidermist's store.

Pechuli was hanging loose on to a duster, when upon hearing the bell he turned around with his hand all the while dispersing the dust particles from the shelves. There he saw Ayda walk in.

"I've come to receive thanks," Ayduk said.

Pechuli detached himself from the dust ridding he had conducted before the entrance of his new friend, and came toward Ayda in a few steps from behind the glass counter supporting, among other things: an electronic till; a cup of coffee or something dark; a pair of eye glasses; a bag made ready for some purpose, most certainly to serve as a means of transportation for one of the products of Pavle's occupation; a small mound of salt (but this way on the outskirts of the counter) and a tomato cut in quarters by its side, resting on a napkin.

"You made the time. I'm glad to see," Pechuli responded, shaking Ayda's hand.

Both men came to a conclusion that, although the time was made on the part of Ayduk, it was as yet too early, as concerned Pechuli, for them to leave their designated place of meeting.

That being said, the absence of patrons was more than visible, a condition, Pechuli said, which was about to be mended, for he was expecting a client at any moment. Having had this business schedule detail brought to his attention, Ayduk suggested that he, Ayduk, should depart from the store, an amendment briskly dismissed by Pechuli who, for the purposes of prolonging his state of playing host, hinted and further expounded on the thought, which he then verbalized, that the two of them should do away with etiquette and remain 'till further in his store, and maybe go for a drink later on.

So concurrent and pleased was he with his host's solution, that Ayduk decided to show a grossly disproportionate amount of interest concerning the occupation of one Pavle Pechuli, i.e. his taxidermy. Asking, inquiring as to the reasons for his dusting the stuffed articles on the shelf, Ayda wanted to know if there was any particular reason for such an activity, and if so, was such an activity common in the profession, and was that the reason why he, Pavle, practiced this activity himself. Pechuli answered in depth and at length, leading Ayda around his establishment, enlightening his new friend on the major points of his trade. Ayduk did notice Pechuli's overly expressed excitement at the mere notion of his, Ayduk's, follow up questions in which he wasn't deficient.

Taking Cooper's hawks, armadillos, boars' heads and such down from the shelves, Pechuli was well pleased with the interest displayed by Ayduk as far as his skill level, criteria and standards he upheld in his work were concerned, which, as he worded, he hoped were more than visible in the said articles, products, whatever you want to call them, he was displaying for Ayduk.

Along the time span of this question and answer period of their meeting, Pechuli mentioned his need to retire behind the counter; specifically he mentioned the sliced tomato and salt mound on the outer edge of the glass surface. Ayda was again concurrent, saying something to the effect of not tolerating food wasting, a sentiment with which Pechuli heartily agreed, already on his way to the place he had designated for his snack prior to Ayduk's walking in, during his act of ridding the shelves of dust.

"You really do have amazing specimens here," Ayda noted.

"They have accrued over the years," Pechuli clarified with a full mouth.

"How many years?"

"Seventeen, I think. That's right, seventeen."

"You said before that taxidermy is an infrequent business?"

"Yes I did."

"How did you manage to keep it afloat for seventeen years then?"

"Exclusiveness."

"Regarding customers, or quality of products?"

"Both. You cannot have one without the other."

The juice of one particular slice of tomato, the third slice, began to drip out of the corner of Pechuli's mouth by way of his chin straight onto the mound of salt in which the slice had previously been dipped. Not wanting any of it, and not lazing about the napkin which was at hand, Pechuli took the paper serviette, and pressed it along the path the dripping drops had made around the cavern of his face, the cavern here being his mouth.

"But there's no one else here today?" Ayda hinted at the further course of the conversation.

"Not yet," Pechuli said as he looked at his wrist watch.

"And it's like this every day?"

"For the most part, yes."

"Pavle, I think I know why you jumped off the bridge that night."

"You do? Why?"

"I think you hate the dusting."

Heads were lowered while the voices were raised. Once the voices were lowered, heads were raised again. After swallowing a near tomato choke, coughing like he did that night together on the river, Pechuli went in the back from whence Ayda heard the faucet letting water, and Pavle drinking some. After an echoing exhale, Pechuli returned, gawking at his tomato slices no more. He took that napkin and placed the remaining slices on it, he then made a sort of bundle of it and carried it to what Ayda presumed and hoped was the kitchen also in the back. Pechuli returned.

"What's going to happen with the salt?" Ayda asked almost too quickly.

In a display of anger broken by a shining forth of an idea delineated on his face, Pechuli turned around and took some sort of rodent from a lower, even-bottomed, shelf behind him. The former animal's stomach had been opened, the thing was well gutted, and Pechuli began stuffing its hollow insides with the remaining salt, the mound of which further lessened in volume.

"Absorbs the moisture, you know," Pavle said shedding light on the point.

Then the ringing was herd at the door anew, and there she was.

"Hi, Mister Pechuli."

"Oh, Miss Lagrada, is it time?"

"Yes it is. As we agreed."

Pechuli made his excuse with Ayda, he held Miss Lagrada in a wait with a kind, reasonable gesture and word, and receded into the back of the store immediately returning with a huge stuffed bird. The man barely made his way through the door carrying the thing in both hands, finally relinquishing it on the glass counter in front of the young woman of a beaming exterior.

"Here you go, Miss Lagrada, your father's peacock."

"He's beautiful."

"Thank you. But I don't think you'll be able to carry it home by yourself."

"Let's see if I can."

Miss Lagrada reached under the belly of the thing with both hands having seen Pechuli bring the bird in also using the whole of his upper extremities. Ayda could plainly see her slightly spreading her supple legs apart, the lace of her garter visible under her opened dress, as if she had carried heavy loads before. She planted herself well, Ayda thought, and not bending her back, but lifting through her bare bent knees, she attempted the lift but failed.

"It's impossible for me," she said.

"I could help you carry it home," Ayda intervened.

"Miss Lagrada, this is my friend Ayda Ayduk."

Not waiting for a response, Ayda extended his hand toward the young woman who took it palm and all in hers.

"My name is Draga Lagrada, and this is my father's peacock," she said as she helped herself with a glance toward the bird still standing on the counter.

"It's a pleasure to meet you, Draga. Do you mind if I try?"

He pointed at the stuffed animal, and after she raised her eyebrows inquisitively he set about what she had attempted earlier. With the peacock firmly in his arms, Ayda rocked it a bit, like you would rock a baby, he did so not looking at Draga who was indeed looking at him, being fed up with the peacock, having failed to lift it herself, she looked grateful as he lifted the bird off the counter top.

"Shall we go?" Ayda asked her.

Draga made her way toward the exit. When she thought Ayduk didn't see her she adjusted her hair ever briefly, no sense in her beauty being obvious, and heard her aid speak to Pechuli as she held the door open waiting for him:

"I'll see you in a while, and we'll go for that drink you promised," she said to the old store keeper.

"Right," Pechuli replied

Having one last exchange of glances with Pechuli, Ayda saw him, of that there was no doubt, he saw Pavle clearly mouthing the words, "You carry it well."

So there was Ayda, carrying the stuffed peacock in both his hands alongside a creature of a much finer plumage. A talk was brought about between them. They were exchanging facts from their respective lives as well as an occasional story they found pertinent to the situation. Along the way, there was no talk of birds.

The sun was shining before them, leaving their shadows behind, beaming upon her as if making her one of its beams herself. She did acknowledge the effect he had on her with a mild but noticeable lowering of her eyes; she did no other things which would make her thoughts and wishes apparent. He did reciprocate by making sure he looked at her often enough. Now, what was 'often enough' in that particular situation when a man is under a feathery load? That 'often' meant he used his eyes, but more importantly he used his words, especially in those moments his arms grew weak. The said words were composed and compiled in such a way so as to leave her without any sense of the weight he himself was feeling which she got an idea of herself at Pechuli's glass counter, as well as other weights of that nature which seem always obvious in such situations. There were none of those.

She saw a shop window, but didn't stop, against her better wish. She saw shoes displayed and summer dresses hung out on hangers outside of stores, but still she didn't stop, even though she wanted him to see her in one of them, which went for the shoes as well. There was something in her step, a way about her walk which she was aware of from before, and she hated the fact that he was unable to see it due to that cursed peacock of her father's. She hated the way the bird made her think about things other than what she was feeling at the time.

In the walk of theirs, and it wasn't a long walk, her building was soon just in front of them, she made sure to asking if he was alright, and she did so in a way that wouldn't bore him or, heaven forbid, make him think she was an overbearing woman. She then unlocked the front door of her building at the ground floor of which, a bit to the side, was a butcher shop of her father, her family's apartment being upstairs.

"Oh good, the elevator is out, once again. I'd hate to let myself go," Ayda said once they were inside. "Sorry to have to ask," she continued, "It's just three flights. Do you think you can make it?"

Without answering, by simply protracting and stretching his mouth downwards making her smile with his fraudulent frown, he brought about their ascent, the three of them, the bird included. During this, there was one masculine point which Ayda made sure to accent. He made no stops or pauses on the stairs landing between floors, hoping she would advise him to do so, which she did only on the second floor, being that it was hers. Using another key she opened the door to her apartment and let him into the living room. The 'damn' peacock, as he thought of it to himself, was put to rest on the coffee table. She had a look at the bird's glassy eyes, at least the one eye she could see, and then left to give Ayda a glass of water. There he made another masculine point when he drank it no heel-taps in one gulp, and she walked him outside of her apartment.

"Thank you, Ayda."

"Don't mention it. I was wondering," he exhaled, "would you like to have dinner with me one evening?"

"Yes. We could go see a movie afterwards."

"I could meet you here on Friday, round eight o'clock."

"I'd like that."

"It was a pleasure meeting you. Good bye, Draga."

"Bye, Ayda."

He started making his way down the stairs when he stopped to hear her close the apartment door softly, and then, standing there, he heard nothing else for a while after.

Draga stepped toward the end of her room, the curtains of which were closed. She was on her way there because she wanted to open them. She did stop however, right near the coffee table, letting her arm enable her hand to provide her fingers the opportunity to thank the peacock which she patted on the head.

"Good job bird," she said quietly.

7.

Draga Lagrada

Sifting and rummaging through her wardrobe, the hands of Miss Lagrada were nearing the second eight hours of that day. The light cotton sweaters were discarded, the shirts of sharp colors rejected off hand. She loved what she was doing, but she disliked today's date making her aware of some of the poorer clothing purchases she had made, though never pinning such sentiments on Ayda who as yet left her door without a knock.

On the hanger up against the side wall of her armoire, an evening outfit found her. Taking it out, that skirt and blouse, she made her decision. Having already taken care of her makeup look, her hair look, she dressed in her Lady's Label skirt and adorned her shoulders and other young aspects of her with her Lady's Label blouse. And then there were the shoes.

It was all fine and well, those colors of summer footwear, but she felt that she needed something more, and feeling so, she thought that something more was needed aside from her own want. So some of her shoes she didn't even pick up, some she just glossed over (one particular pair she glossed over with scorn of a 'what was I thinking' look on her face). You see, she wasn't wondering what would Ayda like, she was trying to discern how would she like to remain in his memory, all be it with a possibility of their get together never again repeating.

Brown, oh please no; red, not yet; pink, maybe in the day time; blue, didn't go with the skirt; black, yes, quite the attack! Black it was.

She was right, as she realized looking at herself in the mirror, the shoes made her skin beam as if the moon was in her room, the skirt giving off such a notion, not her flesh as such; the blouse didn't make her look official, but did give her appearance a serious look, serious in a most desirable way. She was fashioned.

And just as she thought she was early, that she would have to spend a certain number of those tedious minutes at home waiting, Ayda rang the doorbell which she made sure to answer, letting her mother remain sedentary in front of the television set. The woman in question said nothing to her daughter, all she heard was Ayda telling Draga that he had made the reservations, she then heard her daughter shut the door of the apartment, leaving her to wonder as to the end of the sentence "And what about the..." Miss Lagrada was of course asking about the movie they had planned to see later, but her mother never found that out.

They took Ayduk's car to the point of their designated dining destination. Lacking in that overburdening feeling of formal dining, but on the other hand of a pleasant atmosphere and food prepared not too ornately, the restaurant was to Miss Lagrada's liking, a knowledge she made a point of expressing to Ayda immediately after they entered and were shown to their table. The placement of their sit down was also much to Miss Lagrada's liking. Enough people passed by, but no crowd was formed next to her and Ayda. She said it was nice, making Ayduk come to the conclusion that it was more than nice, a thought he stumbled on looking at her thick, wet, lips while she was saying it and having once said it she left her lips rest in the hint of a smile.

Ayda Ayduk thought he could do no wrong, which made him worry all the more. It was obvious that things had gotten off to a good start, a start so good in fact that at one point he failed to see his purpose at the table. The state that he was in however, was relieved by the waiter frequenting the place of their sit down, asking questions and following them up with suggestions of his own. And once Ayda had ordered from the wine list, once they had ordered their choice of dinner, once he saw the look in Miss Lagrada's eyes, the waiter returned no more.

"Do you come here often?" Miss Lagrada asked.

"Only on occasion. I like the food here."

"You look like you don't go out much?"

"Was I clumsy when I asked you out?"

Miss Lagrada took a sip from her wine glass. Not wanting to leave her alone just yet, Ayda did the same.

"No, not clumsy, just…, you seemed as if you were saying something you already knew."

"Do you like your wine?"

"Yes, as a matter of fact, I do."

"I wasn't saying anything I already knew. I was expressing hope," he explained.

She presented him with what remained the most beautiful smile of that evening.

"I'm glad you're honest with me," she replied.

"The truth will set you free, right?"

"No, the truth won't set you free, the truth will obligate you," Miss Lagrada said.

"Then consider me obligated," Ayda raised his glass to her.

"Chin, chin," she said and they toasted.

The waiter came bearing their dining choices on a serving tray refracting the light from up high, from its source in the shape of something akin to a chandelier. The waiter said nothing. Miss Lagrada made sure of that by looking him straight into his eyes. He only relinquished what he had brought to their table, wished them a good appetite, and, Ayda noticed, like that police officer on the river bank that night, he turned on his heels and made his way back from whence he came. Ayda was still pondering on the similarities between the waiter and that police officer when Miss Lagrada noticed a heaviness about him.

"The night is ahead of us, there's not much to remember for now, don't you think?" Draga Lagrada said.

"I agree. It's just that our waiter reminded me of someone."

"You looked guilty as he was serving us, do you know that?"

"That's not how I was feeling, you can be sure of that."

"I am sure. You just shouldn't let strangers know."

"Did I?"

"Hide your sins so they don't mock your virtues," Draga Lagrada said with a laugh.

He looked at what was on the plate in front of him, and as he proceeded to cut the meat segment of the dish, Ayda made sure to raise his eyes and briefly look at the woman he was beginning to adore. Of course he did so at the moment he thought she couldn't see him, herself readying her cutlery for the load of a bite. But she did see him looking at her, and she was glad that look was brief. There was no talk of birds.

"How's your food?" Ayda asked.

Caught between a chew and a swallow which she swiftly deposited into her insides with the help of some wine, Draga Lagrada was made to smile because of the lack of timing on the part of her date. It was then that she knew she interested him.

"The question was put to you too soon, I see that now. That's why I'll continue talking until you finish with that bite. Personally, I always thought well of people who harbor a good, healthy appetite. Perhaps it's a sign they don't feel embarrassed about their wants, their current needs, be they as simple and everyday as food needs. As you can see, I also eat a bit fast, I have no tolerance for lack of freshness when it comes to food. So it appears you agree. I'll take that to mean that you're happy with you meal, both because it was your choice, and because it's fresh food. Good, I'd hate to have that waiter explain himself and the manner of the proprietor's cuisine choices. If you want me to continue I would be more than happy to, but if we're going to make the movie, I should bring my tractate, provided for the pleasure of your chewing in peace, to an end."

Draga Lagrada began to laugh through her smile. And once done with her bite, she had another sip of wine. With a look of a man who had just succeeded, Ayda filled her glass, but not before filling his own. The wine did infuse the evening into her memory. She was still smiling when only one piece of a calf muscle remained on her plate. Ayda, on the other hand, had a choice of a clump of a remainder of a steamed broccoli, and one roasted piece of a forearm. They both did away with waiting, though both of them wanted to stay a while longer. They enjoyed each other's company and she saw the heaviness disappear from Ayda's face, making in her own attire a more relaxed look.

The dining portion of their evening was done, they moved now in image and word to the movie theater, and there they were, Ayda and Draga sitting one next to the other exchanging notions of pleasant thoughts, regarding their sense of each other so far. In doing so, she had noticed one thing. She saw Ayda look at her bare knee once she crossed her legs, which caused her skirt to ride up, making a point of discovering what he was doing without him knowing. Having got enough of such an attentive and somewhat direct gesture on the part of her date, a gesture she didn't mind, she distracted him from turning a soft gaze into a stare with the words:

"Could I have a bonbon?"

Not having wanted to leave anything to chance with regards to the timing of the movie, and therefore having left the restaurant without sampling the establishment's deserts, Ayda was compelled to purchase the sweets Draga was alluding to in her question at the movie theater.

"Thank you," Draga Lagrada said when he returned with a brown bag of bonbons in hand.

She had done it. He had stopped undressing her with his eyes. A trait she thought didn't suite his nature, and though both were sitting comfortably, she was indeed leading him forward as she again pulled her skirt up slightly, brushing off the sugar dustings from her bonbons.

They were well into the movie, it was one of those 'oh, time, do pass me by' kind of fairs when Draga Lagrada laid her head on his shoulder while holding his hand in hers. That's at least how Ayda felt about it, a feeling, nay, a firm belief which was validated half an hour into the movie. Not needing a further clue, and no, this wasn't a thought permeating his mind by means of innuendo, Ayda turned his head atop hers and asked her if she wanted to leave, expressing that he got the sense she did, and reaffirming the correctness of her wanting to leave, if indeed it was so, by telling her that he felt the same way about the movie.

"Yes," Draga Lagrada replied.

It wasn't that bad really, so the latter portion of the evening was brought to a demise, it was a demise of their own volition, it was they who wanted to leave, it was they who made the choice. It remained uncertain whether Ayda was aware of this, but Draga Lagrada new it for sure, they had just made their first unanimous decision. She was well pleased about going out of the movie theatre while holding Ayda by the hand the way she was with the melted lens of her last bonbon upon her tongue.

"You didn't like the movie as well?" Draga Lagrada asked.

"I think the actors were bored out of their minds, and they felt they needed to do something, anything to pass the time, and they did precisely that, they made a movie."

She laughed through another smile, making him give her one caress with his thumb over the top of her hand. Draga Lagrada knew the evening was going to end with a kiss.

Ayda drove her home, he didn't want to make one of those nonsensical stops along the way which would make her remain beside him for that much longer, as neither he nor she were the overbearing type. He drove to where he needed to drive in order to get her home. He so wanted her to sleep and dream of him as soon as possible. He wanted the memory of that evening to become hers as much as it already was his, but being a man he needed no dreams, all he needed was rest , and besides, tomorrow was a working Saturday for Ayda Ayduk.

He pulled over by the curb outside her house that he had gotten to know so well, as he had waited for so long before climbing the stairs to knock on her door earlier in the evening.

"Walk me to my door," Draga Lagrada asked.

She wanted everyone to see, she would make sure everyone know. She got out of his car and stood at the foot of the steps of her building, behind her back there was the dark shop window of her father's butcher store. He saw a calm and stillness in her eyes and in his she felt lightness. He gave her a kiss, and she received his giving one in a manner reciprocal, stalling where their pleasure dwelled.

Draga Lagrada reached into her purse, took out, no, tore out a piece of paper from what Ayda later understood to be her day planner, numbered dates atop, and wrote on it hence handing it over to Ayduk, saying.

"I want you to have my phone number. Here."

He took the piece of paper and looked at those numbers she had written, and there he saw her handwriting for the first time.

8.
Loading Meat

Before the morning was over, and after the learned men had gathered at work, them being two men and one great yanker of chains, meaning Ayda Ayduk, Zokora, and Krot, a new delivery came to the morgue from the police department and the medical institution of the city.

Gathered around the metal slab, the two men, learned men that they are, studied the designated new comer, attired in a beaming, luminous light from the ceiling. All the while, Krot was busy at his desk in the appended room.

The assistant that he was, Ayda mostly stood across the Chief watching and learning the ways of decomposition. There were however moments during his observation of the man conducting his own active observation of the body in which he thought, briefly but acutely, about her, about Draga Lagrada. The Chief noticed his assistant's haphazard absentmindedness yet he chose to ignore it as long as it didn't interrupt their work.

The corpse in question was that of a man. Ayduk thought the man looked familiar to him, and at those times, when he thought that, he would look at the Chief who was looking down at the corpse. The body of the thing was not much, and as such gave off no familiar sentiment in either of the two men in whose stead it was charged. There were no marks whatsoever, no discerning scars, not a single hint of life, a life lived, you understand. He looked quite sterile.

The former man's bones appeared to have been an accident of birth, their developing into a structure, that is, a structure that never should have been. They were just 206 lucky draws. The Chief noted that the corpse's skull was bumpy, very much a relief, though he didn't write bumpy in his examination report, he wrote bulbous, doing so after feeling around through his hair, a right sculptor shaping his clay. Continuing with his examination of the rest of the axial skeleton, and having briefly turned the corpse over on his stomach, the Chief paid attention to the man's vertebral column, and, rolling the corpse over again he did so with his rib cage. Zokora was visibly bored.

"Natural death is tedious," the Chief said.

Ayda didn't respond. He didn't see the Chief's words as his way of breaking the silence, bringing about the discontinuity of the boredom that surrounded him. What is more, the Chief didn't notice any kind of reaction on Ayduk's face to what he had said, prompting him to restore that which he realized his assistant interpreted as a rhetorical remark.

"This would be a good time for you to add your thoughts on the subject."

"What?" Ayda said as if coming to.

"Do you find natural death interesting?" the chief reiterated.

"I don't know."

"What are you, some sort of nut who works toward a state of inactivity? By rigor mortis, man, don't work only for the grave."

"I agree, Chief, my mind just wandered away for a minute. Do you find him dull, as well?"

"As dull as an old man's after lunch nap," the Chief explained.

"Look, even his irregular bones are regular."

Zokora laughed and noted his assistant's findings, writing down his last remark as concerned the corpse's skeleton. 'Till further they continued their study, and as the Chief suspected through his original claim, his conclusion was that the man died of natural causes.

"Krot, when's the meat guy coming?!" Zokora shouted to the kid at the desk.

"At ten, as always!" Krot replied in a shout back.

"Ten o'clock! But it's..., what's the time anyway?!" the Chief shouted again.

"Fifteen to ten, Chief!" Krot's shout back answer was heard.

"Oh..., good. Ayda, let's wrap everything up before more comes our way. Do we have everything?"

"Yes. The organs are neatly organized in the freezer, the lab work is negative, quite innocent on all counts, the measurements have been conducted. That's it."

"So, now we wait? Krot, how much longer?!"

"Five minutes, Chief!"

Ayda retired to the toilet to relinquish the tides of his bladder. The morning was nearing its first interlude, and with it the Chief neared the appended room where Krot was sitting in business on his Krot-like chair, at his Krot-like desk, when the young man yawned.

"Didn't you get enough sleep last night, or is it too soon to ask?" the Chief, the right den mother, asked.

"I was with my girlfriend last night."

"Oh? Really? Your girlfriend now?"

"I was throbbing for a bobbing, Chief, I had no choice."

"Krot, you really are a perverted little corpse to be."

"What isn't crazy has no psyche, Chief," Krot, the big yanker of chains said.

"But it does need rest," and there that discussion ended.

It was at that point that Ayda Ayduk returned, he was all 'what's going on here' and 'boy, did that feel good' looking like a right-binary fellow. And upon his return he informed his colleagues of a distinct ringing at the back door. After acquiring Chief's gaze, and wondering why there was no gaze acquisition from the kid, he did put Zokora's amazement to rest regarding the passing of time which that one always eagerly followed, making it pass slower, hence the observation.

The Chief rushed toward the back door, rushing his subordinates along with him. He motioned both wings of the exit and entrance asunder and reaffirmed both his trust and belief in Ayda when he saw the meat guy. There he was, the meat guy, casually looking at his work order, as if not even admitting of a possibility that there was a chance the door wouldn't be opened for him. Although dressed in overalls, he had a look of a man who knew he was needed, a right symbiont he was.

"By rigor mortis..." the Chief began with the criticism.

"Right on time, Doc," the meat guy didn't even look at his watch.

"There's not much today," Ayda intervened.

"What can you do?" the meat man replied. "Now, if you will, gentlemen – to the meat," and the meat guy made all of them turn on their heels, and followed them into their place of business.

"Are you still with that girl, Krot?" he inquired from behind.

Was the meat guy chewing gum?

"We don't trade in our own stiffness. You know the rules," the great yanker of chains said bringing about a brief silence.

The silence brought about by the great yanker of chains didn't last long, seeing how they were soon in front of the metal slab surrounded by a metal wall of metal doors resounding in their dead metal sheen which was barely a sheen; it was more like a mat surface giving off light.

From there Ayda and Krot began loading the corpses into the truck out in the back while the meat guy went over the day's load with the Chief.

"All the meat is sound?" the meat guy asked.

"It's always sound from here, you know that," Zokora should've had another cup of coffee.

"I know nothing, Doc. You should see the types I have to do business with."

"So you want empathy for your paranoia?"

"How's your boy to girl ratio?"

"Traditional," the Chief replied.

While all their leisurely linguistics were on going, two men were actually working. Loading and unloading corpses from their shoulders, Ayda and Krot were moving back and forth between the morgue and the truck parked in the back, a truck manned by another Krot like counterpart, very much a young man, though not as young as Krot, who had in his charge the business of receiving and hanging the bodies brought to him into the back of the meat man's truck. They, the two men, Ayda and Krot, didn't talk to him, they were just dropping their loads into the open rear of the thing, and before they could perceive him as something more than the recipient of their labor, they would turn their backs to him with only the young man's huffs and puffs behind them.

They don't know how many trips they made; it couldn't have been more than five each, since, as Ayda had said, it was slim pickings that time. But there were occasional exchanges of looks and not-so-good looking glances, sharpened in all parties present in the transaction for the purpose known only to men of different cohorts whose professions and work only crosses paths out of necessity.

In such conditions of mutual understanding and tolerance brought to bear, the only one calm and collected was Zokora. In and of itself this came as no surprise to his side, for they knew the Chief had nerves of steel, steel in the form of iron bridge cables, they were also in the know about what could happen when cables like those are under too much stress and strain that they break, which is why Ayda made sure to get the job done quickly, as he was able to hear, at least in part, the conversations between Zokora and the meat guy.

On their last trip to the truck, carrying a load of a he and a she, Ayda and Krot were accompanied by the Chief and the meat guy. Upon their farewell the men of the morgue noticed that the meat guy apparently had no relationship with the young man who was obviously in his employ. Of the three gentlemen this fact angered Krot the most, and the way he was, the great yanker of chains, he began to stare at the meat guy who was going through his list with Zokora before he closed the back of the truck. The meat guy eventually noticed the kid's chain yanking eyes, and being a man distinctly bigger in built than Krot, he made his way toward the back of his truck. Krot didn't budge an inch, and he was in the right for not doing so. The meat guy said to his aid to vacate the freezer now loaded with meat, and Krot's opposite number jumped out of the back and immediately made his way to the passenger side of the truck. The meat guy then shut the freezer, turned around and gave the kid a long, kind-of 'I'll see you next time' look.

"I'll see you on the hang back, sir," Krot said as he made his way back to his desk where the phone was ringing.

The truck departed with a frustrated sound, and seeing how those were modern times it even left an aroma of tenderly refined gasoline behind it, making its frustration emboldening to the observers. It was truly a respectful gesture, with its rear displayed for them and all.

9.
Drinks with Pechuli

Ayda and Pavle met on their lunch break; oddly enough they didn't meet for lunch. Along the way, each of them in his own manner pondered on a thought of the morning past. Though those thoughts were two quite different notions of the time which had elapsed, they had shared that time and shared it apart.

When he was near the place of their meeting, Pechuli felt his stride prolonged as if something wouldn't let go of the sole of his shoe. Upon closer inspection, prompted by a squishy, squashy sensation, a discarded chewing gum was made visible to him. Pavle then briskly began rubbing the shoe, the sole of it that is, against the pavement in an attempt of ridding his gait of it, the gum that is, ever glancing ahead to where he spied a vacant table at the afore-agreed-upon café. For a brief couple of steps he remained walking by dragging his foot, or more precisely the shoe on which the chewing gum was stuck, relenting from the operation only after the chewing gum had done likewise, and was pulled from the sole of his shoe.

The table contained prior helpings of former patrons the establishment had catered to, which he didn't like. At the outset those red lipstick smeared tall glasses, coagulated remains of their cappuccinos, their state of aggregation changing before his eyes. A solitary hair certainly departed from a balding head lay on the table right in front of him, between his arms resting on the table's surface. Pechuli looked around for one but he saw no waiter. He was no longer expecting Ayda, though he was indeed curious as to his courtly advances to Miss Draga Lagrada of which he was as yet uninformed. And then the wind gusted in a current, making that retired human follicle stand as if to attention, swaying until the unsustainable gust had past.

As he waited, people past by his seated person, though his eyes bore no resemblance to a man in the middle of a wait, let alone to a man expecting to hear the news from his friend. No one looked at him, it was as if all who passed by knew of his jump from the bridge, and thought of him in shame, but Pechuli didn't care. There was still no waiter, there were only those remnants of someone else's leisure time in front of him. It was as if those objectified offerings for the sake of future mercy and perhaps the ever expected repeating of the sit down were somehow increasing in number and expanding in influence in his mind. It was then that Pavle Pechuli got up and went to the bathroom of the local.

With the same intention but from another direction, Ayda Ayduk made his way there too. He was making it in such a way that he himself wasn't aware of the fact that a table had been designated for him by his friend. Unlike the party waiting in the café, Ayda was present of mind and that mind was presented with ideas, concrete sentences, on what he was going to impart to Pechuli concerning Miss Draga Lagrada, not because he was a man smitten too soon, but simply out of knowing that Pechuli already expressed interest in their walk, their date, and in all with the moments and exchanges between Ayduk and Lagrada thus far. But there was something lacking about Ayda, he felt as if his arms had no strength to them, in fact it was simply the residue of the release of strain from when he put down her father's peacock on her coffee table. It was then, on his very approach to the said café that Ayda smiled unknown to anyone.

The two men did finally meet at the table of Pechuli's choice, one after his arrival, the other after his return, only now the table had been cleared. With a distinct raising of the eyebrows into which Ayda didn't inquire, Pavle gestured to his friend to sit down, and they began to pass the time in chit chat, while in earnest both were hoping for the appearance of that rarest of animals in these kinds of environments – the waiter.

A disillusioned optimist is a person well on their way to becoming a cynic. Having said that, rather than hoping for the hapless young man or girl to inform them of their beverage options, Pechuli began asking Ayda about his first date with Draga Lagrada, and he knew he had hit the mark, i.e. that his questions were exactly that about which Ayda wanted to talk about when he saw the man from the morgue grinning like an idiot. Soon after things were brought to a sentiment much more real.

Ayduk talked at length about the date and Pechuli listened completely devoid of strain, not asking question regarding matters about which his friend obviously felt strongly. Then came the present time and the much boasted about past morning, and while the two men were at that point relating purely through their own professions, Ayda noticed a steaming boil in Pechuli's eyes. Ayduk's talk of the loading of the morning's corpses and the meat guy seemed only to make his listener, Pavle's, feelings all the more expressed on the rest of his face, delineated with shadowed lines, brought about by the dreadful service of the establishment and all associated with it. Why he didn't just get up and leave was beyond Ayda.

"The waiter will be here. Relax," Ayda tried and missed.

"Thanks. By helping me, you're actually helping the waiter."

Out of the glass, wood, and metal door the waiter busted out like a race hound, only this racing hound had no charge in his eyes. He settled his aggressive legs at the side of their table.

"Are you gentlemen ready to order?" he asked.

"What is this? One of those 'no man is an island, but still we don't care' kind of places," and that was Pechuli restraining himself.

"Quite, sir. If you're not ready to order..."

"No, no, we'll have none of that. Write this: one black coffee, and..., Ayda, what'll you have, coffee too?"

"With milk," Ayduk said.

"Write this: one coffee – black, and one with lack of black."

"That would be milk coffee, sir?"

"Yes it would," Pechuli said.

"Would you care for anything else?"

"You have our order. Be quick about it," Pechuli said as he rested in the chair.

"I shall have to ask you to wait faster, sir," the waiter responded, exhibiting his lizard-like shoulder blades shaping his vest.

Looking at his friend all bothered beneath his collar, Ayduk said, "Let's change the subject before the subject changes us."

And though it looked as if it was too late for Pavle, at least that was the case at a glance, Ayda didn't let go of the notion that there was still some calm in those waters. He began telling him again about Draga Lagrada, but this time he was telling the story of their first date through her perspective, at least how he saw it or would like it to have been. Rare were the instances in which Pechuli, an otherwise calm man, even more so since having survived a jump off the bridge, would retrace his raging and enraged steps back to the skinny, grinning waiter, but those instances did show, and they were obvious to Ayda who was determined to play the role of a peace maker, so Ayduk said, "To ill consume is to ill conceive."

All things considered, the man of the morgue was laying it on pretty thick, the things meaning a bright sunny day with only a breeze to worry about. Eventually Pechuli resettled in his place of former calm now made present by the fact they were served by a completely different waiter, in fact the new waiter was so different that Pechuli even managed enough calmness to notice that the aforementioned hair on the table before him was also gone, and must have been for some time. He thanked the man, whether it be he or not, for clearing their table; he was presented with a courteous smile of a man who then turned, much like his coworker before him, making his way back into the local, not busting through the door.

"So, have you seen her since," Pechuli asked.

"Yes, in fact we've been out a few times."

"It sounds like things are improving. Before you know it you'll even have real regrets."

"Do you want to hear a joke?" Ayda asked.

"Yes."

"What does an architect call his dog's house?"

"What?"

"Bauhaus."

A light intermission was instilled in which laughs were exchanged, making Ayda think he should precede.

"Do you want to hear another one?

"Okay, but I liked the first one," Pechuli said.

"Two bullets meet in mid-air, and one bullet goes to the other, 'So, they fired you too?'"

He damn well busted a gut, Pechuli did, and whereas before no passersby noticed him, now people were turning their heads in passing, happy at the sight of him, the ones relaxing in the local did likewise. And yes, comments were heard, and transfers of looks and glances were made, but Pechuli didn't mind the scene, it was as if he had never been waited on before.

"I have to go to the bathroom again or else," he said, and Pavle did go, laughing out loud all the way.

Finishing his milk coffee, having put down the cup back on the saucer, Ayda motioned the waiter who served them, and once the man approached he was given new orders of drinks, "Two sodas, if you will." On his way back, Pechuli was in such a good mood that he said, "Hey!" to the waiter leaving Ayda. Pavle's eyes were beaming, his forehead was clear and tight and then and there Ayda knew what his friend was like as a young man.

"Oh, how did this place become so nice in the end? Thanks, Ayda; I think that's twice you've saved my hide."

"Don't mention it. And please don't spread it around, I don't want things to be expected of me."

"Oh, hog wash! Besides, I think Miss Lagrada saw right through you."

"No."

"'My, how lovely he looks stuffed and mounted over her fireplace,' is what they'll say about you when she's done, he-he!"

"And that's it?"

"That's all that there ever was."

10.
Loveforging

Having parted ways with Pechuli, Ayda Ayduk returned to the morgue. There he found that the business of the day had continued. The Chief and the kid were accepting new arrivals and Ayda found, once he was there, that he was more than needed. Afternoons were always busier, none of the men questioned why, they just accepted it as the norm in their job. Zokora had his own thoughts on the matter and the question why that was, but seeing how all three were well along in the day of work, he expressed nothing on the subject, by the look on Ayduk's face he knew that it didn't matter, not enough to dwell on in the middle of the work day anyway.

They settled into the hours which were passing ever faster. It was obvious they were well in stride of labor, not thinking about time. Krot gave his usual excuse as to why he wasn't able to tend to the new arrivals by sharing his thoughts on the business of answering the phone. The Chief didn't give it a second thought because he had no first opinion on that subject, so he relieved the kid from what was in fact manual labor, continuing to note what Ayda was telling him upon his ever-repeating arrivals into the room accompanied by either a police officer or a medical professional.

Yet once there broke a certain time of day, a time designated for the conclusion of labor, at least for now, while Ayda was elbow deep in a cadaver, that Krot came to the door of the room with an insufferable grin on his face. Of course, Ayda didn't see this, and why should he have, determining a person's cause of death and everything, when the kid came in, and approached Ayduk, shamelessly ignoring the Chief standing at the side and monitoring the work of his assistant.

"A young woman's here to see you, sir," Krot grinned.

Ayda looked at Zokora as if asking permission to end work for the day. There was no female face visible from behind the glass portion of the door; she wanted none of those sights. The Chief told him to finish up, saying he should be able to do it quickly, and much to his surprise after listening to his boss, and not arguing with him, Ayda did finish up, and he did so quickly.

"I'll see you after the weekend," Zokora told Ayduk.

Not knowing why, before going out to meet the woman in question, Ayda made a point to take off his examiner's attire. Though he didn't know who the woman waiting for him was, it was more than obvious that Ayda was hoping it would be Miss Draga Lagrada. Once in his normal, bloodless clothes, he made his way through the door, with Krot following him in stride. It was her, he saw her clearly looking at the bulletin board in the hall as if marking what it was that her boyfriend was exposed to during his usual day on the job.

By detaching her gaze from the pinned paper pertaining to pertinent prescriptions for that day, she turned his way, softly stepping across the linoleum of the hall, well-lit by the neon encased in a plastic casket above.

She said she came to see where he worked. She said she wanted to surprise him. She said she had no plans for the weekend. She said that she hoped she wasn't interrupting. She said she was hungry. She said she knew of a place they could go. She said all those things, asking nothing, and reached out and acquired his hand in the end.

The two of them disappeared behind the front door of the morgue. They took Ayda's car to a restaurant near her home. There was an easy silence throughout the ride and a sensation on their tongs perceptible only at those times one of them would speak. She told him he can park in front of her building, and when she heard him inquire as to the whereabouts of her family's car she informed him that they went out of town for the weekend. My goodness, the clumsy look that man's face expressed, he should've seen him go ahead with his parallel parking, but there was no way he could've avoided that question, he wasn't hinting at anything, nor was he hoping, a right man, a right pollinator. Good for him.

Their dining choices bore no great significance, but they did order desert, a point of the menu accented by Lagrada. So they were served two slender plates of sweet which was one of the rare things in their city not containing meat. She knew from before that he felt uncomfortable feasting with her on bygone bodies, that there was an unexpressed but paradoxical holding back each time they would sit down for a meal, and now she saw Ayda relaxed, she heard his voice give off a lightness of thought. He made her laugh, which she would always only do through a smile, her teeth mostly closed.

They finished with their courses of choice, she giving him a look, and he getting up from his chair first after having paid the bill. Because he parked in front of her building, they had to walk that way anyway, and in doing so she took his hand apprehending his nerves and making them yield to hers. She was right to do so, and Ayda felt it too, on the other hand, he wasn't able to explain it in this way, but he did feel her manner before anything even happened.

He saw the door of her building, and she took a short lasting look at it as well, but unlike him, she had an expression of a native of a city looking at the postcard of her home town, for her it was just a way in, something one goes through without thinking, or as is common, thinking but only in retrospect. But she was presented with a slight problem, she needed to say something to him, she didn't want them to go through in silence. Without much thought, and in utter absence of strain, Draga Lagrada looked up to the sky, spying a luckily solitary gray and stuffed cloud formation. And yes, it might have looked like a pretty weak excuse, telling him it's going to rain and that he should therefore come inside with her, and him admitting to her of not wanting him to drive in the rain storm.

"It is Friday, you know. There'll be traffic, and nervous people at the wheel," Draga Lagrada had said to him.

Which was not necessary to say, since he accepted, supplying her with a smile that didn't look like the grin of a confused idiot anymore. Their hands parted on the approach because she reached into her bag to get out the keys to her building. None of them minded that climb up the stairs once they got in. Ayda was following her on their way up, and the destination of that way up had its place at her door. Yet another key was employed in the discharging of yet another lock, all those locks being hers. Letting him inside only after going in herself, a soft merging of the entrance/exist and its surroundings was heard on her floor, if the neighbors were careful enough to listen.

Behind the closed door her heels were resounding on the wood floor, leading him in and showing him the way, they stopped, those sounds of her footwear, not long after, because her apartment wasn't big, and carpeted in places. And on the window pane in her room the first marks of rain did appear as she had hoped they would. With this, their scene was camouflaged from the eventual view of the outside. And of course that eventual view was further put to sleep once Lagrada drew the curtains shut.

The rain created a kind of membrane on the surface of said window; whose drops followed into each other in a seamlessly confusing order of patterns. The only thing that was certain were the marks the drops left behind. Softly slipping in their dripping, they were accruing on the bottom of the outer frame of the window, and after a brief gathering of the water mass, the collected liquid dropped down, doing so along the surface of the outer wall of the building. It was as yet imperceptible, but the material of the house's exterior did vesture itself in a slightly more closed shade of its original, intended color, as it became wet. The majority, or the better part of the water mass presented in such form currently didn't make it all the way to the ground, for it was soaked up by the wall, but it did have a purpose, that disappearing of those first charges of the liquid, and that purpose was precisely to saturate the dry surface so that the following water mass would indeed make it all the way to the ground, and unless the building were to have grown legs, to run out from the rain, that cycle could not have been avoided. But even if it did manage to develop a means of escape, wherever it would flee, it would still get wet, depending on the size of the storm, or at least a storm no house could outrun. So, it was, put in its place, remaining thus to serve the purpose for which it had been built. And truly, as time elapsed, doing so ever faster, the more the rain came down, the walls were given a helping of one shade after another, while those same window panes admitted to no view from the outside. That being thus, the storm turned into a true downpour, the contents of which managed to reach the ground, proceeding to course and flow in an unnoticed stream toward the bottom tilt of the building, showing the water mass the way along its sloping pavement where it did imbue and infuse each and every crack and micro-chasm of space, the walk and its curb provided. Moving on its way, the water mass met with the edge of the gutter, and in a purling cascade it fell down into the drain and continued to course to wherever the drain was intended for.

It was one of those summer rains which never seem to stop; it gave the city cause for pause, and brought down the swelter which had been beaming down to where now were streams in the road and the hidden sounds of streams between the buildings, hidden by the ever ubiquitous drumming of rain drops upon their place of stay. Everything was gray and dimmed, there was nothing for anyone to see, the drumming drops hid the moans and other articulations from within, verbalized in a rare coherence, and sounding whispered, "You're my spark in the dark. You do know that don't you?"

The passersby were turned into runners along, and as Lagrada mentioned before, there was a nervousness among drivers, which was manifested in the sounds of halting car horns and the screeching of brakes, the sliding of wheels and such. The greenery in the street was the only thing thriving. For the first time in as many days it all looked fresh, not bothered, and not frustrated, the leaves directing their own kind of water mass collected by means of their own growth, and they directed it downwards to where their roots were. From outside the place of planting, at the outer edge of the sidewalk, meaning the small, designated plots where those trees stood, water worms began surfacing, making their way for whatever purpose and reason, i.e. nature guiding them; where they made those running along look ugly, slimy and disgusting.

The slithering nether ground of those afore mentioned drains began to raise its level, its opposite number; the drain pipes on the buildings supplying the watery stuff, giving it cause to serve, the only ones enjoying that scene being the people who drew up plans for the drainage of the street. They were surely smiling, barely able to wait for the downpour to pass so they could come out and inspect the correctness of their many plans.

The sky was coming ever closer to the ground. There were shapes of wet and shapes acquiring wet in their descent. The expanse, the breathing room, if you will, was given content, it's as if there was a merging of the opposites in a way quite concordant. Dusk was setting in too. The moon was shy that night, all it gave off is a refraction of the star from across the way. Beaming down what was imparted to it, the cratered conductor of the tides was softening the look of the scene, giving off light through the clouds dwelling above. Those clouds were brought into a state of a settled motion too, meaning there was movement to them but it was as if they wanted to hang around and stay put. And while their bellies were dark, those sides of theirs exposed to the moon were lit up as rarely seen, showing the rain the way down to the buildings, the streets, the pavements, the gutters, the drain pipes, the runners along, the water worms still making their way up toward a rest earned from their flooding tunnels.

The stars remained hidden. It's not right to watch a heavenly body wash and refresh itself, and she did so effortlessly, though there was no breeze, no wind in her surroundings, she was at times provided with breaks to gather up her strength and proceed along her designated cycle. Those breaks manifested themselves with the change of the density of the thing falling down, washing her, and though the rain did start innocently, there were off course changes and alterations in its intensity. Through it all she didn't fight it, but she didn't surrender, because the rain was in her character. Hence the heavenly body reigned in her abode, recharged, having given charge, and eventually the moon became clear above, the clouds stopped their loitering over the city, in the end there were no streams and courses in the streets, now they were all underground.

Inside all was calm; the man was resting in her bed while the woman wearing only a sheet made her way toward the window. She pulled the curtains apart and opened the panes, accepting the fresh, cool air into her room where he lay. Dawn was braking outside; Ayda knew that because her hair gave it away. Not taking advantage of such cognition, he just smiled, well pleased with himself. Draga Lagrada went to make them two cups of coffee, doing so without asking first. She stepped over their clothes from last night, scattered on the floor, and found herself in the kitchen, tending to the brewing beverage.

Once more by his side and within his reach, Draga Lagrada put forth a motion of the two of them going to a pastry shop of which she knew, and having got Ayduk's consent, she went about the business of day break.

11.
Meat Packers' Alley

Her business of day break included a face wash, a look around the mirror's within, a teeth brushing and the appended proceeding brushing of hair, the securing of her bra, slipping on fresh panties and generally dressing, a return to Ayda, now well on his feet and dressing as well, the closing of the window, the brace up of the strap of her bag, a turn toward Ayduk buckling his belt, saying, "Let's go eat."

It was still early in the morning's rise, but they knew a stroll would keep them in good time, not too early so they would be met by the closed door of the pastry shop, and not too late, oh to imagine, so they wouldn't have to wait in too long a line. In going outside with Draga Lagrada, Ayduk barely noticed his car parked where he left it last night, as if forgetting it was even there. She made a mental mark of that. There was a coolness about the streets they traversed; there were people along a beaten path, beaten most recently only last night. The leaves on the by the way trees were bloated from the rain, the soil of their flora's foundation was soaked, leaving the prior cracks in the once dry earth merged in an affordable softness of mud. Last night's rain worms lay still on the pavement due to the lack of liquid, the morning sun shining along their way, bits of them squashed and smeared, on the pavement itself, some from the possible shoes of those former runners along.

Their walk came to a traffic light, and upon relenting their motion on its red shape beaming from a well-positioned form, both Ayda and Draga were afforded an opportunity to see three figures on the other side of the street they were about to cross. Seeing only the figure in front, for those people stood one behind the other in a row, they were made aware of their nature only after they began moving into the crossing of the motor way upon the turning of the shape depicted on the traffic light, turning in color and position from the aforementioned red to a new green. Ayda and Draga commenced with their traversal of the motor way heading to meet and pass by the three figures. Only now that the light was green and they were able to cross did they clearly see the humorous scene of two young mothers pushing two strollers, one behind the other, each with a baby making their lulled-way across the street. The young mothers held their heads upright, not in a manner proud, they held their heads upright, positioning their lips into two equal hint-full smiles of knowing. Behind the two women in charge of the two babies, a garbage man followed, pushing his garbage bin containing his broom and shovel, he held his head bowed touching a loose and exemplary relaxed collar of his jump suite with an utterly serious countenance, serious out of confusion, you see, his lips were pouting just like the babies', and his eyes, though cast downwards, were indeed sulking with no charge in them.

That's how Ayda and Draga went into Meat Packer's Alley, a procedure in which, one should add, Draga smiled at her mate who reciprocated by taking her hand in his, leaving her mind to rest in the search for the answer to the question, "Now, where is that pastry shop of yours?"

Meat Packers' Alley wasn't as long a street as one might think, but it did demand of the ones walking though it a certain sense of the origins of cuisine. In those early morning hours, like the one in which Ayda and Draga found themselves, the alley was filled with meat in the first stage of packaging, therefore there were bodies displaying shades of skin and turns of flesh hanging on bars which stood on movable wheels, like the ones you might, nay, you can find on a suitcase. The bodies hung on racks. The aforementioned sense of the origin of cuisine, and of course the various dining preferences thereof, that one might not even think about in the morning, were made more than obvious to Ayduk, walking as he was, alongside Draga Lagrada. The man gave off no discomfort, and she should know, he divulged no impending looming gloom because of the scene of meat packers carrying their designated portions into the buildings at the side. On the other hand she didn't make light of what she speculated was his first time in that street, telling him things like how her parents used to take her to this particular pastry shop when she was a little girl. How the owner of the establishment was good friends with her old man. In general she spoke about things from her memory, making him perceive his obviously new surroundings through a view quite richer than just dietary in nature. There was one other reason why she chose to take him specifically through that street, the cause of her initiative to do so was rooted in the conflict she felt in him that time when he walked her home carrying her father's peacock. Back then she was made sure of his sense of humor, and of the latent lightness of his overall character, not just one trait of it mind you. On the other hand it was more than visible to her that Ayda was a man who acted and behaved in a manner somehow foreign to his nature, as if he had imported certain beliefs a long time ago, or, to put it in a more understandable way, she was sure that he had been pitched to, and she knew that he had bought the pitch, hook, line and sinker. But knowing that, there was no sense in her going about changing a man the way he was. There would be no point in attempting a change in someone who, due to the purchase made, was made unable to interpret the things in his own life correctly. It's not that she thought he was attired in a burden of sorts, although she was quite sure that he did import or purchase said beliefs. She did notice a behavioral mechanism in him, in other words, she found, and had determined this with a great amount of certainty, that every time he would come across a brilliant idea, and express it even more amazingly, he would always, as a rule, follow it with a laugh at his own account. Draga Lagrada knew that this was a man who nearly debunked himself from existence. She felt very pretty while in that walk of theirs through Meat Packers' Alley.

Those aforementioned behavioral mechanisms of Ayda Ayduk that were happening right before her eyes, those tools of his, that unconscious acquisition he had made, were finally becoming his environment. For the first time since she had met him, she saw him in his element, coming to such a conclusion based on the things he was speaking of and the ways he spoke of them. Being in that alley, he was brought back to his nature, and though there was no obvious logic to him, no grand philosophy, there was a towering presence of common sense, that which gave people fire, that which gave people the wheel which had indeed been turning in Ayda, and only now he boarded. In doing so, he was riding himself of his mental crutches, and nothing gave way, not one aspect of his person expressed the slightest fear or discomfort, not because he wasn't aware of what was going on, but because for the first time in his life Ayda Ayduk realized that he wasn't guilty, nor was he innocent.

To make better use of his newly remembered original state, a state therefore conditioned with acceptance and rejection of said guilt, Ayda began looking around, and with Draga by his side the way she was, made certain points on the road ahead more clear to him. She felt as if she had been hiding all her life until now, and the perpetual siege mentality of her former state of mind was being made to disappear. In finding himself, Ayda freed her, but if there had been no Lagrada, he would never have had cause to search.

Ayda Ayduk saw a man walking their way, half-way toward the pastry shop; it was his neighbor Mister Balaban. The old man had a look of frustration from negotiating the meat-filled alley, which Draga Lagrada recognized, having lived in that siege mentality herself all her life. Mister Balaban's state of mind and condition of body were made more than clear to the young couple when Ayda explained the figure coming toward them with a curious set of featured feelings delineated on his face, he told Draga that he wanted her to meet him, though it was common knowledge to both of them by now that Mister Balaban was frustrated and might not give leeway to a conversation this early in his day. Ayda brought him within reason, and from the outset of those first utterances, Mister Balaban became present in the day.

"It's good to see you, sir. How are you, Mister Balaban?" Ayda asked.

"Ah, how must I be?"

"Please let me introduce you. This is Draga Lagrada. Draga, this is my neighbor Mister Balaban," Ayduk said as he made the introductions.

"It's good to meet you, sir," Draga responded

"And what brings you two here?" Balaban said answering a point of his own inquiry.

"Were just on our way to get some pastries," Ayda said.

"Ah, breakfast! I knew I was missing something. Thanks Ayda. Miss Lagrada it was a pleasure meeting you, my dear. I must be off, I just remembered something..., what was it again?" Balaban said as he touched his chin with a finger nail that needed trimming and cleaning.

"Well, we won't keep you, sir. And it was nice meeting you too," Draga Lagrada said.

"Of course, I remembered, they're paying out pensions to-day! Much obliged, young lady. Now I really must have to go. And Ayda, I had no idea you got so rich overnight, congrats."

After giving off a smile he would realize only later at the post office while waiting for his pension check, Mister Balaban continued on his way, his 'I really must' procrastinated into the oblivion of the remaining stretch of Meat Packers' Alley he had in front of him. The couple didn't stay to dwell on the walking away portion of Ayda's neighbor, and so Ayda turned his side, his better half toward Draga Lagrada, who then acceded to a further step meeting his own in a kind of cartel action forward.

Mid street, within a few steps of the place where they would breakfast, the couple discussed that which was pertinent in their morning, a morning with a dawn quite lagging behind, making them therefore feel quite peckish especially after a bit of faster walking. And so, as the velocity of their steps met with an in-crease, their tongues behaved in quite a different manner, they grew slower, in other words Ayda and Draga talked less. A thought less significant than the look of them, passing as they were along-side trucks in a fracas, vehicles of various sorts with their gears in neutral, and their handbrakes in park, and a common place shout making way for tasks at hand, loading and unloading, among the men working in Meat Packers' Alley.

And there it was, hidden just on the corner at the very end of the street, the delicious pastry shop of her childhood which La-grada had spoken. It stood well-adjusted to both its surroundings and its purpose. The look of the thing was appealing, a point in fact made obvious to Ayda, who was there for the first time, by an abundance of patrons entering and exiting, in all directions, frequenting the pastry shop.

Draga Lagrada didn't let him hang around the shop window to build urges when an appetite already existed. Not that Ayda suggested such an outlook, but she didn't want him to regress now that he had progressed. They got in quickly, overwhelmed by the aromas and the smells of the air streaming from the kitchen in the back, aromas which weren't deficient in the display cases as well. People making purchases were waiting in line. Others who already had gotten their orders and were served, were sitting down at tables, some engaged in a chewing chat of sorts.

The couple made their way to the back of the line. Ayda was ever propping himself on his toes wanting to get a better look at what was on offer in those display cases. Of course whenever Draga Lagrada would take a step forward, seeing how the line was moving along, Ayda was brought down to the ground, his heels, arches and all, to step alongside her.

When asked by the young girl behind the counter about her pastry of choice, Draga Lagrada admitted to no confusion or ignorance, giving voice through the lexemes, "Two kringler, please."

Wrapped in wax paper, Draga Lagrada was given her helping of two kringler, who briefly displaying it to Ayda, gave a look about her of a hunger about to be deposited beneath a sediment of sweetly baked goods. Having taken the said goods in both of her hands, and the payment was made by Ayduk because those hands of his Draga Lagrada were full, and there was no sense in making a task confused to boot. The couple then found a table for themselves, where they sat down and remained so in silence, eating the delicious, knotted, sweet bread. Quite the breakfasting man he was, she thought. Ayda Ayduk that is, as only he made comments on the food, and this because Draga had frequented that place often, unlike him, an exile in his own hometown, going around doing nonsense like trying to untangle a weathered knot with his tangled fingers and such. And not being able to refrain from speaking about the more than obvious aspects of the bake goods he held, he made sure to do it under the power of his voice. Draga Lagrada was in comprehension of this and she reciprocated with a short lasting stillness of her jaw and the appended jaw muscles, providing him with such a smile which only she knew how to provide, you know, with her eyes. She knew she would never get tired of him.

12.
Next Door

The night came mellow, and in it Ayda came back home after escorting Draga Lagrada to her apartment, leaving her in good spirits and making sure to depart without giving her a sense of being left behind.

By way of his car, still parked where he had left it the night before, raising his head toward her bedroom window, he saw her light go on and her curtains go shut, she had well-earned sleep coming. He got into his car, subtracted it from the side of the pavement, and off he went upon meeting the road with the rubber of its tires.

Divided by a blinking strip of white, a stretch of the motor way designating for passing and taking other motorists over, he made his move against a quite nonfunctional city bus which was just plodding there in front of him. He would've had to pass the bus either way but having gone about it the way he did, Ayda avoided the sounding off of the car horns of the drivers behind him in a neighborhood where Draga Lagrada was meeting her day's end. Even then, he wanted to give her no cause for too early a rise.

Continuing in his drive, Ayda could've seen alongside his passing a narrow stretch of sidewalk ornamented with various people, some passed out against a fence, some being passed over by a rare pair of sober legs, he could've seen all that but, the sound and responsible participant in traffic that he was, Ayda chose to look ahead where the traffic lights were turning colors from red to green, gesturing the way of his choice toward the place of his rest.

Outside of the aforementioned parting of the couple, a parting marked by a much clearer distance now made available to Ayda at the wheel, and Draga on the pillow, there wasn't much else noteworthy or worthy of any notable mention. However, as he was running low on fuel, and yet the engine, the tireless thing, persisted in its motion, only hinting at the state of its tank, its gas tank that is, with an occasional vapor tremor under Ayda's foot on the gas pedal.

Back at his building he had no sight of his or his neighbor's window from the front, for the building was placed with its windows, the main ones anyway, toward a modest court yard in the back. The neighbor in question, of course was, Mister Balaban whom he and Draga had met in Meat Packers' Alley that morning. Concerned about his state of mind as well as the outcome of his wait at the post office, Ayduk decided to bring his evening to a close with a light, polite conversation with the elderly gentleman living next door, with whom Ayduk had shared that particular floor of the building ever since he found employment at the morgue, upon graduating from university into a much more demanding manner of study.

And in such a manner, which he came to learn a bit along the way, through a bit in wandering, Ayda Ayduk got into his own building, letting the door retreat to its original position behind him by means of a mechanism installed at the top of the frame. Giving off no sound, the door simply brushed the floor attired in a carpet path leading ahead toward the profile of the elevator by which Ayda walked, and having done so, he let his stance remain in an erect upright position. While upon pressing the button the elevator shaft descended in a sort of light. The light of course belonging to the elevator itself, as is always the case with matters in motion, be it linear or lateral, up or down, and every which side of way. No one was in it when he opened the door, letting himself in for a ride up to the next door apartment. The jerk of, he supposed, the elevator cable, yanked forth a stoppage in his ascent determined by his flight of choice made obvious by a lit button on the panel inside the elevator which went out after he opened the door again.

There was a shout while the door retreated toward its closed position, a shout echoing in familiar words, familiar to all who live among people like themselves.

"Hold the elevator!"

Out of surprise of not anticipating such an occurrence, rather than out of fright of the shout itself, Ayda turned and skillfully and effortlessly halted the motion of the carriage door, holding it open for a student neighbor of his who accepted the gesture well in stride, i.e. not giving up on his run toward the elevator which would have otherwise sunk beneath the feet of the young man's expectations of a ride.

But all such frequent notions aside, Ayda reviewed what followed next. First he knocked on Balaban's door, and once he heard the key turn the lock and the lock turn knob and the knob turn in a hand on the other side and the hand make a doorway for Ayda to view his neighbor, Ayduk knew that all went well for his neighbor, Balaban, at the post office that day. The old man didn't hide his appreciation of Ayduk's gesture, he knew Ayda didn't come asking for things as next door neighbors usually make a tedious habit of doing, and once Balaban heard Ayda ask as to the goings on in his day, the neighbor asked him to come in, repeating the operation of letting him in, only now in reverse.

Ayda couldn't recall when he had visited Balaban at home last. The apartment looked familiar, he wasn't mistaking it with a kind of change regarding its interior, nor was he ever prone to forgetfulness of such depth that he couldn't recall a place he once visited. Still Ayda was tired. Mister Balaban noticed that fatigue on his face immediately, hence asking him if he would prefer coffee or per chance a cup of black tea, though the end Ayduk got his way in the form of a glass of cool orange juice. The drained fellow would've gladly drunk the whole carton in one gulp, luckily his glass wasn't much to speak of, size wise, so he was able to restrain his thirst in accommodating sips continued with proceeding accommodating sips.

The evening swelter was in the apartment, the old man didn't like to air it out, and Ayda noticed the fallen rain had given way to a streaming through a much wider bed, he knew that she had kept the rain in her room, which suited him just fine seeing how he didn't want her to have any of that suffocating stuffiness outside of the light of day. He also noticed a transient source of a cool air stream, not knowing why he didn't do it before, he now turned to the direction of its origin and found it, the origin that is, standing upright in the corner of the room, with a caged propeller for a head, turning gently and thus giving off cool air. It was a floor ventilator he had spied, the cursed thing barely noticeable standing in its corner. Ayda asked Mister Balaban why didn't he bring the thing closer to the, let's say, middle of the room, surely, Ayda thought, he would get more out of it. The old man, as old man often do when explaining points of their perception of air temperature, shrugged his shoulders and said that it was too cold for him when he would do so, meaning he had indeed tried it, but in the end his love of the stiff heat, perhaps brought about by his poor peripheral circulation prevailed.

"That young lady you were walking with this morning, what does she do?" Balaban asked.

"She occasionally tends to her father's butcher shop."

"She has no education?"

"No, no formal education."

"How did the two of you ever manage to match up?" Balaban asked.

"I suppose we managed it once the match was made."

"I don't mean to pry or assume…" Balaban began in apology.

"You needn't concern yourself. We simply met, that's all, and neither she nor I took it for granted."

"How do you mean 'for granted'? Do you mean it was love at first sight?"

"I suppose."

"There is no supposing about it. Well?"

"Yes, I guess you could say that it was love at first sight," Ayda admitted.

"At long last, it understands, ha-ha-ha!"

The two men were brought to an upright position, and at the kitchen window at that. You see, there was a clash of two night time joggers beneath a lamp post in the street. Neither Balaban nor Ayda knew what could have possibly brought about such a collision. Mister Balaban opened the kitchen window and they heard the two individuals in a shouting match, all through panting and gasping for air due to them having ran thus far. It was an unfortunate meeting, of course, as with all things, nature finds fortune in all, and that night that particular fortune, the one of a comical scene, was afforded to Balaban and Ayduk who heard, among other things:

"It's only common sense that if we drive cars on the right side of the road, we should walk on the right side of the pavement!" said one of them as he notioned a system.

"Bull! You know very well that what you're suggesting makes no sense at all. Or do you have such a high opinion of yourself that you perceive an engine laboring in your ass!" the other amended to the notion.

"You wouldn't know an engine even if an Englishman built it!"

"And you are somehow an expert on sidewalks?! No wonder, you're probably all about your precious side walking, bumping into people your sneakers find fitting!"

"I had the right of way!" shouted the man with the plan, i.e. theory.

"There is no right of way in pedestrian traffic!"

"What traffic? May they traffic you to your grave!" the man premising said.

"Don't make me count your bones where you have none!"

"I'll disregard my fitness and give up my evening run just to consign you to the pavement!"

"Make sense already, why don't you!" the man defending himself from the premise said.

"Sense is readily available if you wish to accept it!"

"I'll do anything to draw out your attack, to make you break that posture of yours!"

"Well then, by all means, do!"

And upon Balaban's yell of "Gentlemen, please!" the two men, both at once noticed a light burning in the old man's kitchen and the old man himself with Ayda by his side, an Ayda who was looking on at the scene of panting anger and frustration which he didn't understand, for he knew from experience that the sidewalk was wide enough for a city riot, let alone for two men to run along, and this was confirmed with his view from above.

"Now, if you two will be on your way!" Balaban commanded from his position.

And they broke up the clinch to be, each going from one another, and further running in his own direction. Balaban explained to Ayduk that this was not the first time he saw them jogging past each other, it seemed to the old man that the two gentlemen in question favored this corner of his concrete abode for reasons he never understood. Ayduk had never seen them before, and relinquished all further thought on the matter by finishing off the little orange juice left in the glass he had carried with him to the kitchen window.

Ayduk left Mister Balaban's apartment an hour later. There was a slumbering lull on his pillow waiting for him upon his retirement from the day as yet to pass in a lowering of his horizon's view. Leaving his clothes on the floor like he did last night in Lagrada's room made him recall the light state he was in back then, and having thus retraced his steps in his mind and wandered to her lying, waiting for him, naked, the moon glistening on her pale skin, he fell asleep.

13.
Equal Parts

Sunday was up next. Ayda Ayduk woke up well rested, and in the other part of town so did Draga Lagrada. There was a light interlude in their midst, a midst now somewhat apart. Once up from his bed, Ayda walked into the kitchen. Upon spying the door of his freezer, he reached for a glass up in the cabinet hanging on the wall. With glass in hand he employed the kitchen faucet and poured water into the glass, and further in the sentence drinking it with waking thirst.

It was not a working Sunday, as if no man would die that day. The phone didn't ring on the stand by his couch. There was neither a knock nor the sounding off of the ringing bell at his front door. It was very much a day about which, as Ayduk concluded, nothing could be done.

There was a newspaper lying in front of the door of his apartment, and in that newspaper a piece of information caught Ayda's eye. The advert announcing that piece of information talked at, or at least hinted at the possibility of a trip, a vacation if you will, that was how Ayda perceived it. As most media do, the ad in question suggested an affordable parting for Ayda and his usual ways, the stalemate into which he had fallen, Draga Lagrada not included, and in fact explicitly excluded. His first thought was to call her up and proposition that the two of them should take the trip together, but he knew they've only been together for just a short while, so he did away with such childish notions of the latency within him which was quite romantic.

But he called her anyway, as she was the one who had given him her number, provided with a notion that she had indeed woken up and was well out of bed, a fact which proved true once he heard her voice. It was a mutual exchange of morning greetings, and a kind reverberating in a copper stream of sorts, in which Ayda expressed and Draga received, doing so without judging him, or retreating to her suspicions as becomes a person in a relationship who is provided with an illusion to do so.

He told her of the newspaper ad. After being asked as to the specificities of the possibility of the thing he was talking about, he reaffirmed her hopes that it was only a matter of the possibility to rest. In response, Draga Lagrada gave off no suggestive expression, as one would find in a sigh or a change in the tone of voice, its color and content, she was in agreement with him all the way, in that he should take such a vacation if he so needed. She only wanted to know when would he be back in town, and, all previous lots being true, she was given an answer, putting her forward time in a more recognizable state.

The phone conversation between Ayda and Draga ended as it began, with no surprises, no expectation of turmoil or shock. The cards, both their cards, were on the table, and there were no secrets or want to be secrets between them. To prove the validity of this claim, it only has to be noted that after retiring the receiver of her phone, Draga Lagrada was prompted into a decent stretch, bending over to touch her toes, and then lifting her bare leg to her ear, making her further step toward her kitchen much limber and relaxed, and therefore making the business of that day, at least as far as she was concerned, of the same nature.

After getting off the phone with Lagrada, Ayda called the number of the company advertised in the newspaper to which the ad was pertaining. Provided with all the necessary information of his unplanned but broached undertaking, Ayda Ayduk said, for he got their call center on the phone, he would be in their customer service branch on Monday.

It was all well and good for him to want to take his vacation now, but he had made no prior arrangements with his employer. Suddenly the prospect of his trip began to hint at a cadaver-like outlook. Ayda didn't want to wait, and being next to the phone already, he dialed the Chief and got an answer right away. He was given permission to take off, of course only after providing his boss with the same piece of information relating to the time of his return he had provided to his Lagrada.

With everyone clued in to his sudden Monday plans, suddenly there was a busyness about his Sunday, but it was a busyness not rushed, it was as if he had tapped into a source of energy reserved only for him, and it was as if all the people he told of his plans were in the know about such source.

After finishing with his shower and shave, or was it a shave and then the shower, Ayda Ayduk enacted a decision to go out for a walk. In doing so, surprisingly he met no one in the hall of his building, neither on his floor nor in the lobby of the thing. The first thing he had to do outside was to go around a line at the news stand where the people, about a dozen of them, were waiting for, what he supposed were lottery tickets, as the newspaper had reported that the scheduled prize was near a record amount. Putting aside his preconceived notions about the poor habits of his fellow citizens, Ayda made way for a further step, having gone around the end of the line they had formed.

His curve, the curve of his forward motion that is, ended up on a straightaway stretching out until his sight was met with a turn of the sidewalk. Ayda had forgot to bring his wrist watch; it seemed he had dressed inadequately that morning. Sundays, go figure! Notwithstanding a prospect of being outside without a sense of time, he found many time pieces and time keepers in his vantage, some in windows of stores, some on poles alongside the pavements end, so, in general, he felt that he did alright time wise.

Putting such pressures aside, the pressures of lacking in certain aspects of the space he was traversing, he found that the passersby made for quite nice studies. Everyone seemed to be rushing somewhere; it was as if they had all turned into news bearers of sorts. *Do imagine*, he thought to himself, *the average Joe was in the know!*

Ayda didn't care for the destination of his morning walk, it wasn't what people called a constitutional, he didn't care because necessity didn't make him care. Regardless of the fact he had yet to purchase the ticket which would take him on his vacation, his trip had already started. In fact he damn well nearly busted a gut upon the sight of a street corner busy of men talking nonsense like 'invoices' and 'pro invoices.' Ayda conclude that it must often rain in their offices, and that there was snow in there too in the winter. He further questioned how those creature got anything done at all, and then he saw a byway beggar sunbathing his palm, and said to himself, *Oh, so they get nothing done, in fact.*

Such was the conditioning of that day, he guessed. It was all so old, the sight of those guys, it was all so unbearably archaic, anachronous, and even, continuing with the prior observation, retarded as far as Ayda was concerned. The scenes of which he was able to get a glimpse provided nothing but confusion, in a confused mind, of course, but Ayduk's mind was no longer confused, it was the belabored individuals, their posing strain, their ever-present false hunger to present themselves as worthy of their ambitions which came to the surface.

He could even find humor in what he saw, and that humor didn't delineate on his face. Maybe he knew it, or maybe not, but Ayda already had become an ace. There was however one thought that did manage to break through in Ayda's mind, a thought untainted and unsoiled by what he saw around him. It was a point in fact brought to his attention upon passing along two of those belabored individuals, the only thing tough about those two men were their haircuts, crafted it seemed to Ayda by a welder. The thing Ayda heard was a question asked by one of them, overburdening Ayduk's airwaves the way they were, all out of place and by the look of them definitely out of time, the question was one concerning the meaning of life. Not being able to help but ingest the proposed sentence, Ayda Ayduk picked at his molar, a tooth of his, with his toothpick that he had just for the occasion. You know, he said to himself, leaving the two belabored individuals further in their dark, "The meaning of life is a life with meaning."

He thought his answer was as appropriately simple as was their question. As soon as he came up with it, he ceased with any possible updating of the thought, making a group of pigeons pecking at he didn't see what in front of him, strut away to the side, or more accurately to two sides in any case, *roo-roo-rooing* their way toward the edge of the sidewalk on one, and toward the base of the window of a shop on the other side.

Leaving the simple tones of the simpletons behind, Ayda Ayduk surely made his way behind the aforementioned turn of the sidewalk, while the street itself had the option to continue in a straight or sideways direction. The mellow yellow was well in its rise, as Ayda headed forward, so did the sun proceed by way of the Earth's orbit.

Getting out as he did, his wallet from his pants pocket, he counted the money he had with a glance, remembering distinctly where he got it, seeing how he had just spoken with his boss on the phone. Acceding to a shop which had a counter window in its build, Ayduk designated the amount of bank notes needed to purchase salted sun flower seeds. The little bag of no more than a few handfuls bore a makers mark, and Ayda tore at it, beginning to nibble on the stuff which he got by means of the opening he had made as if he was sitting on a park bench of sorts and not out in his walk which began to lead him through the much nicer part of his neighborhood.

Mothers were out walking their newborns, the fathers were, as Ayda assumed, at home tending to their television sets, as it was a Sunday, you understand, and the games were on. There were kids playing hop scotch on the sidewalk where he made way for the continuation of their pastime by bringing an arch into his step which lead him around their fun and near the curb of the pavement. The Sunday stores were open, that's what made them of a Sunday kind, there were no lines in them, no one had to wait, they had week days for that sort of thing. Bicycles were being ridden on the motor way itself, where there were yellow lines on it, designating the portion of the pavement meant to serve the exercise of the bicyclists. Ice cream stands were speckled alongside Ayda's walk which was nearing, as he discovered, its destination, of which, as mentioned, he wasn't aware of before.

Ayduk's view opened up to a small park placed in a snug of someone's plan, the city's plan, you understand. Green of leaves, the chestnut trees grew between benches on which people were sitting, the trees roots sinking into the ground just beneath, while the yellow mellow was beginning to beam down unprovoked by the summer calendar. Pigeons were pecking in a prerequisite of their nature that which was left from the breakfasts of those breakfasting on benches.

With the bag of sunflower seeds in his hand, Ayda sat down on one such bench. He will further remain there, sitting as he was, nibbling on the flowers not to be, until a true hunger will drive him back home for lunch, or maybe he'll be forced go to a restaurant, he's not sure – he never is. Those walking like he used to were now passing him by. He saw tough shoes and sandals, and he was met with sounds of heels too high for that time of day. They must've been returning from someplace. There was the creaking of a nearby kids' swing and the thumping grounding of a portion of a seesaw going down and pounding into the dirt, and the rest was yet to be made true tomorrow when he would go to the travel agency from the newspaper ad.

Time will pass, everyone will live and grow within or without, either way it will happen because, as Ayduk realized looking in front of him, nothing in life is a given, nothing is just understood.

14.
Favorable Conditions

Monday, Monday. *Time to get on board, my dear Ayda*, and so he did, having purchased the tickets, which were in his respective inside jacket pocket, while in his hand, goodness only knows which one, there was a suite case ready to go, as ready as he'll ever be.

Quite the dull mechanism, the airplane that is. He had already arrived at the city's airport. Anywise, quite dull, in all, all of the tin and much like a can of a soda beverage which, by the way, they did serve during his flight. But no, Ayduk wanted a beer, but the precious airline, as precious as an airline can be, had no beer to serve him, so instead he had a fickle little fizzy-fuzzy drink, presented to him in one of those plastic little cups, the kind that take forever to decompose in the earth.

But the less said about the means and manner of his transportation the better, for Ayda Ayduk had other things on his nervous mind. The things in question included:

1. Item one: Did he or didn't he cancel his subscription to the newspaper.

2. Item two: Did he set the affordable temperature, affordable to the meat of course, on his freezer.

And:

3. Item three: What will Draga Lagrada think of his sudden, unannounced and abrupt departure?

She, like most things always and forever for weighing on his conscience, was the item with which in his mind Ayda's plane departed from the tarmac of the runway.

Enough with modes of transportation and alike. Enough with the virtuality of human misconceptions, the passenger turned his attention to the gallery of characters present aboard Ayduk's row. Present was a man, of a quite unbeholden built, sitting by the aisle; a woman, sitting by the window drawn half-way down by one of those airplane blinds, and Ayda, the nervous man of the morgue right between them, as if unwanted neither by the earth, nor by the sky.

Aside from his tier of placed seats, of which there were three, for Ayda traveled Economy class, behind the back seat of the place of his seating there was an obnoxious child kicking and flouncing about his back's rest. The child in question, as Ayduk supposed, was surrounded by its parents, a suspicion, for he had many of those, made more than true upon Ayda turning his head, ever so politely but briskly to the left, to let the threesome behind him know of his uneasiness with the position he was in, an uneasiness made all the more true by the aforementioned kicking and flouncing he felt mid-spinal column. And upon doing so, in turning his head over his seat to the left, Ayda Ayduk saw a man, a youngish man, fit for a pollinator, but, on the other hand, not so much for fatherhood, because in that brief turn of head, Ayda saw that man looking into the ever closer clouds whilst, on the other hand, rolling his eyes at the behavior of his child which was, in fact, as Ayduk was brought to realize, playing a game of sorts with its mother. Surely it must've been with its mother, seeing how our man of the morgue heard a notion of a woman's voice coming from the opposite side of Ayda's head turn, she spoke bellow the power of voice.

Across the aisle, all in chuckles and smiles, was an elderly couple. The elder man was seated nearest to the pass-way, to which Ayduk immediately thought of the man's resemblance to his neighbor Balaban. Anyway, as far as Ayda could see, or spy (quite the curious inquisitor he was), the elderly couple was chuckling at the instruction manual, one of those quasi-laminated things kept in place by a rubber band on the back of the seat in front of you.

The others present on board were not much, not much for sake of mention. Still Ayduk went over, and did so briefly, through the remainder of the gallery of characters present, this of course outside of his peers' cognition:

Now the usual passengers in the Economy class are comprised of stuffed people, stuffed by what's in front, way in front, behind that magic velvet divide behind which there is, yes, the Business, and further, yes, the First class. All in all, Ayduk considered, they sate as it had been designated to them by the airline of their choice, an airline of which he shall not speak at this moment, for Ayduk began with the mention of those aspiring ones of whom not all were stuffed, not before the time of the flight's meal.

There was a chuckle behind a buckle, and not the one of the aforementioned elder man. There was a snicker of a lollypop licker whose sex we shell leave undetermined, since it was undeterminable to Ayda, though at best guess it was a man parading as a woman. There was a snacker of a peanut bag already cracked open for his or her pleasure, again whose sex was unclear, this time in part due to age. And amid all these sky-bound people Ayda Ayduk sat calmly, begrudging the lack of the option of having a beer on his, this unplanned, flight.

In such a state of sit and wait, bound by nothing but his own pre-seeded notions of what a trip should be, an air trip, that is, the man of the morgue proceeded in his seat, now in a laid back position and pondered on the things he would do and places he would visit when he gets to wherever he was going to, a location, as before, not mentioned to anyone thus far.

At the optimal altitude the serving cart began making its way along the aisle. It was all the usual air fare food, some in the species of fish mongers and a variety thereof, some in the species of chicken breeders and a variety of choice of cut of meat, as Ayda understood: breast, drum stick, etc.

In any case the little cart, pushed by an elderly steward woman, her uniform thirty years worn, made its squeaky way along the passage, amid the passengers on either side of its metallic loins. The woman asked and the flying bunch received what was their tray of choice – fish or chicken. And no, none gave voice of complaint, none except our man of the morgue who, due to his as yet not coming to terms with his other-than man-eating habits, chose, and he did so right in between that aforementioned gentlemen on his aisle and the after him mentioned woman by the half-shut plane window, a kind of vegetable sandwich, you know the kind, all in dressings of salad, tomato, bits and bytes of salt, pepper and whatever one might find in such a diagonally sliced piece of soggy bread-in-between.

So there he was, no one above and, as much as he could gather from such an altitude, no one bellow him. But still there was something missing. There was the lack of the icy cold bite in his sandwich, the ready dead, readymade meet from his freezer. And he remembered, thinking to himself, *What was it she said*, 'Hide your sins so that they don't mock your virtues.' And other such thoughts came coursing through his mind in the thin air, like, for example, the words of his neighbor 'Your will meet your burn', and his reaction, a reaction utterly abrupt and, from this height and this perspective of a not-that-bad a cloudiness, for it was sunny in flight, now such an unexpected one on his part, unexpected for he began to make peace with himself. Do imagine, a man making peace with himself.

And all the stuffed birds of a pretty feathers he had carried within, and especially the one he carried for Draga Lagrada, i.e. her father's stuffed peacock, as if livened in the aspect of their wings.

You see, the cabin pressure must have been too low, and at that time of that present, he had nothing to show, but to present the aforementioned vegetable sandwich again and again to his mouth by way of his laborious teeth.

Once more to the brink, dear Ayda, and so it went for the duration of the entire flight, a duration in and of itself not lacking in the usual plugging up of Ayduk's ears and the curious sensation he got in his stomach, then half-full from the vegetable and goodness knows what kind of bread sandwich. You see, the aforementioned sensation was caused by the airplanes gradual but steady descent during which the man of the morgue had fallen asleep, awoken by the gut feeling mentioned above.

The thing that woke him up as well, and this was the thing which brought him into the state of being present in the day, for it was daytime, was the opening of the airplane wheel shafts below him. At that point Ayda turned to the woman left of him:

"Are we landing?" he asked.

"Yes, I believe we're about to," the woman replied, looking out through the blind on her window the full way up.

Ayda Ayduk looked up at the lighted display showing him to put on his seat belt, which he did. There was a murmur among the passengers, as is usually the case before plane wheels touch tarmac, which they do eventually, but not before Ayda looked at the man to his right, still fast asleep as he himself was not just a moment ago.

"Sir-," Ayda said having nudged the gentleman. "The lady says we're about to land. You really should put your seat belt on."

"Thank you. Is it time already?" the man replied.

"According to the woman in the window seat it is."

"Thank you madam," the other passenger addressed the said woman, "I almost landed wayward."

"Think nothing of it, sir," she replied.

And with that brief interchange of words presented through a dialogue quite outlandish, being how the plane was indeed about to land, the wheels of the thing did indeed touch the runway, but it was a different kind of runway in a different kind of place where our Ayda Ayduk would get lost to the world until further notice.

15.
Conditions of Family

Now, not much was mentioned of Draga and her mother, the absent minded woman, absent minded with respect to her daughter, notwithstanding her husband's stuffed peacock still adorning their coffee table of which she, the mother that is, found out that it was brought by one Ayda Ayduk.

She was a woman of her own nature, Miss Lagrada's mother that is, a nature so alien to her daughter that they barely spoke among each other. This, and this alone is the reason why her mother did not bare a name in Ayduk's understanding.

Perhaps because of the way and under the conditions she, the nameless one, met her husband to be while they were going out, perhaps because of her realizing that she was to become the precondition of the Lagrada family herself, once the matrimony was more than obvious and, to use a phrase of an archaic coinage, 'in the cards'.

Cards, do imagine! As if a woman's future is determined by signs and symbols, and not by the make of her maturity, for everyone knew that women mature faster than men, but dependent on what.

The nameless mother, nameless only in her first name, so to pay respect to a woman who had given life and hence he called her Mrs. Lagrada, the other one Miss he supposed, would spend her days outside of the outside, meaning she mostly lived indoors, spending her time in front of her TV set, herself not knowing what she was watching on the screen radiating waves of length and goodness know what sort of strength.

Occasionally Mrs. Lagrada (that's agreed on); occasionally she would take interest in her husband's work. But Mister Cosimo Lagrada didn't like his wife hanging and loitering in his butcher shop next door. Mrs. Lagrada was, it seemed, a woman chased away from whatever she wanted to get close to in her life.

But she did adore that stuffed bird, even though it would obscure her view of the television set from her place of siting on the sofa resting against the back wall of the family's living room. Imagine, she, and this was noted by Draga in passing, when she would pass on her way to the bathroom, she, the same woman denied, would stroke the tail feathers of the ever shining peacock on the coffee table, shining even in the glow of the cursed set, sitting on board a chest of drawers of sorts.

Mrs. Lagrada was all in the know by now of the place of business of her daughter's boyfriend, his boss the Chief, the great yanker of chains kid Krot, but what couldn't put her mind to rest was one other simple question: 'Why hadn't Draga brought him over for, let's say, dinner.' You see, you see, that's where her suspicions lay with regard to her daughter's choice of mate.

"Have coffee with me, I'm on my break," Cosimo the butcher would ask Mrs. Lagrada. But for lack of him meeting her half-way in the manner of his own work she would reply "I've already had my coffee, remember, I suggested it to you earlier and you said now."

Cosimo Lagrada was the one of the two of them who would get up early in the morning, for the opening of the shop and the preparation thereof. During this time, Mrs. Lagrada would remain alone in their matrimonial bed, only with the footsteps of her daughter pacing through the house, nervous for the Mr. Ayda Ayduk that had disappeared, as well as her voice while she would confer with her girlfriends on how, why, and when he had decided to make himself absent and lost to the world.

"Mother are you listening in on my phone conversations," Draga Lagrada would ask upon her mother's waking up.

"Stop talking nonsense!" Mrs. Lagrada would reply.

All that is fine and well, but they did have a good rapport when they were just a young mother and a young lady to-be. It was more than obvious that that had changed somewhere along the path of matriculation of both mother and daughter. A man builds, a woman creates. So which one of them chose to be the latter, and which one chose to be the former. It was, of course Miss Lagrada, for Mrs. Lagrada had decided to model her character after her, back then, husband to be, for Cosimo was a no nonsense man, a true builder of things he himself didn't create, a point Draga Lagrada hinted at to Ayda on their first date if he could recall her words, dared to repeat them in this context.

Mrs. Lagrada was, in a sum of words, a character of a woman as still and auto-repressed toward her daughter, as that stuffed peacock seemed to be. It seemed to be so, but only within the nuchal bone of her skull. As most things ordered that wise, it was as yet to come to the foreground of her as a wife, her as a mother, but only later, and later is precisely called later, because later is always too late.

So, father would tend to the food, the meat from his shop and the vegetables from the farmers market, Draga would study with him at the butcher's, learning the trade herself, for, as becomes a woman of youth and beauty, she had ambition in her, the aforementioned creatress in her.

One might even call the relationship between Mrs. and Miss Lagrada one of plagiarism. Ayda would have gathered by now that, in the case of their own inter-dynamic, it was the mother who envied Draga. And she would show it too, he knows, making herself all pretty, hairstyle-wise, just like her daughter.

It went as far as Mrs. Lagrada synchronizing her nail clipping, both of hand and foot, with the same operation her daughter would perform. The poor mother was, in fact, trying to remember how it was that she had taught her daughter all those things.

From dress-make, dress up and dress down (meaning Draga's dietary habits, in regards to her figure), Mrs. Lagrada, through the stalemate in her own life, was trying to remember the way she herself was once some short time ago.

And absentminded due to his occupation, Cosimo Lagrada played no great part in the upbringing of Draga. Again, to use an anachronous and even retarded phrase, he was the apex of an absent fatherhood, which is precisely what drew young Draga to her father, and, later on, to his work, the allure of something made mysterious and exotic precisely due to the absence of him from her life during Draga's childhood.

But then again: *childhood-mildhood*, or as the saying goes "youth is forgiven". What is life brought to bear on a child when its surroundings are as yet not blunt and dull enough, and its spirit as mild as a chick's fluffy underbelly? Get your finger out of that *nosy-wosie*, but by all means do nibble on the whitewash on the corner wall of the living room. In the case of the Lagrada household that corner was precisely at the point where the kitchen met their living room.

The tyke Draga used to indulge in such activities too, the bobbing for buggers, and munching on the crunchy edge of whitewash made soft by her saliva and made even whiter by her baby teeth.

At that point and time she was, without knowing it acquiring immunity, both from bacterial and other infections, and, as she was as yet to realize, from the infectious influence of her mother

Bringing this brief of a family build to a close, it would well behoove Ayda to say a few words more about what he saw there, and so he shall: the TV set remained radiating; the dresses were put on and dressed down. Mother knows best, but only while she has a child, and Draga Lagrada was a child no more.

And yes, the peacock stuffed by Pavle Pechuli, carried into and onto the Lagradas' home and coffee table by the now not-present Ayda Ayduk was still there.

16.
Love or Lust

"Krot, where's Ayduk? It's past eight of clock?... Krot?!..., where is that kid?"

And yet despite Chief Zokora's best morning voice, there was no answer, there was just a rude echo throughout the morgue. So, being as he was, the Chief started searching for that ever-damned tinned packaging of his morning beverage. He checked the metallic cabinets hanging adjacent, or rather, above the kitchen sink, but his precious tinned morning fellow-friend was nowhere to be found, so the Chief kept repeating to himself, doing so below the wave length of his mind, "By rigor mortis, someone will be examined for this."

Just as Zokora was about to proceed with his search for the, it seemed, ever-absent tin can, as absent as (and this the Chief was going to learn only later) Ayda Ayduk, there was heard an opening of the door of the morgue, and as he was in those working mornings, the Chief proceeded from before, only now in full voice and at the top of his lungs:

"Krot!!"

In a brief inter-midst of the passage of both time and the kid's footsteps, the young Krot felt his heart begin to race, as he himself was racing to meet his workday's beginning. Krot was late that morning.

"Sorry I'm late, Chief... It was the weekend, you know, and I..."

"Yet another sleepless night, aye?"

"I was throbbing again, Chief, and, well... You know, quite an insatiable girl."

"You truly are a prickled pickled pucker, Krot."

"Well, Chief..."

"Where's Ayduk, where's my assistant, where's my coffee?"

Perhaps he chose the road less-traveled, Chief."

"Less, less! Oh, by rigor mortis! Will you just see about the coffee so we can get on with work?"

The young Krot didn't even get to relinquish his work bag onto his desk where he would normally answer the telephone, so there was heard a thumping drop of his strapped satchel, which he would carry every morning, even on those working weekends, after which there followed a rummage rumpus of a stumbling search in the places that the Chief had already searched for his precious coffee.

"No, Krot, I've checked there myself, it isn't in that cabinet. Try again."

The kid was beside himself, having mentioned yet another sleepless night and henceforth in him, Krot that is, panic ensued, a kind of panic which can bring one to a state of saying something like:

"You and your coffee, Chief!" which Krot did say.

"Never you mind about me and my coffee. And I'll deal with Ayda when I see him. Which brings me to my previous shout out while you were not here: 'Find out where that man is in the meanwhile...'"

"Here it is, Chief," Krot said as he emerged from that exact cabinet.

"Oh, by rigor mortis, you've found my coffee!"

"The metal of the cabinets looks just like your tin, it can be confusing sometimes, you know, Chief..."

"Yes, yes, the cursed things all look alike."

"Moreover, they are placed in to orderly a manner, have you noticed that?"

"What, Krot, have I noticed what!?"

"The manner of the order of the aforementioned cabinets, Chief."

"Listen to me kid. I'm only interested in two metallic things in this morgue. Number one: the metallic thing in which they store my coffee, and number two: the metallic folders where our meat is kept. Give me my tin of baked beans, and I'll get the pot working. Krot?"

"Yes, here you go," the kid answered, handing Zokora his can of coffee.

"Not that you fickled fucker! The phone on your desk is ringing. To work, to work, it's half past eight of clock. And once, if at all, you can find your way to your workstation, do as I asked and call Ayduk. How am I suppose to work without my assistant?"

"You got it, Chief."

Stumble he did, Krot that is, stumble and fumble, mumbling something bellow the strength of voice. It must have been some with regard or at least pertaining to Zokora. Once at his desk, young Krot could clearly hear the pot streaming in a wave of electric charge, you know, to get the coffee going.

"We do have a new filter installed, don't we!?" Zokora shouted toward the direction of Krot's desk in the room behind the doors, as metallic as the rest of the morgue.

And sailing across the down-below of those swinging doors, across the Veronese green linoleum, and therefore softened by it, there was heard an answer:

"I'm on the damn phone. Check it yourself."

"What, what?"

And having put the caller on hold, most probably the meat guy who was about to come and collect his daily load, Krot answered, this time more timidly:

"Yes, Chief, we do."

"A-ha! By rigor mortis, your right. Never mind, carry on!" Zokora shouted.

Still at his behest, Krot could hear the joyful murmur of the Chief waiting on the coffee pot to fill, but, while at his duty, all the young man could think about was the night before, and what a Indian summer night it was: moist, damp, in all hard, as hard as he was while with her in bed.

"Ayduk isn't answering his phone, Chief!" Krot shouted after a brief pause, a pause from his job, that is, in which he was trying to reach the assistant.

"Not now, Krot, not now. I can see the pot filling up. But try again later!"

"You see, all those previous exclamation points of mine were due to the swinging metallic divide being closed."

"I understand, will do, Chief!"

It was at that moment, or to speak otherwise, at one of the points of that moment, that there was heard a familiar buying ring at the back door.

"Chief!" Krot shouted to the attention of Zokora.

"Not yet, the pot's almost full with coffee!" there was heard a shout back.

"But Chief, the meat guy is here!"

There was a lull of sound of the dripping of the coffee being made for that morning, preceded by the Chiefs brisk but soft, soft because of the linoleum footsteps, and the swinging metallic doors were swung open with Zokora remaining in their in-between.

"What time is it?" Zokora asked the one who held the receiver covered by his other hand.

"Nine in the A.M., Chief."

"Finally, someone to show up on time today. Leave your phone business and let him in. And seeing how Ayda isn't here, you'll assist in the loading today. What am I saying?! I'll be assisting you. You see what I mean about never-the coffee. It's a cursed beverage, I tell you. It seems I have to fight to the Gods to have mine in peace. Now, hop to it!"

And hop he did, rushing in a wrestler's run down the hall toward the back entrance of the morgue where, indeed, the meat guy was standing as young Krot made sure to the fact upon opening the door. And there he was, as it seemed to fit him, again in his overalls with pad and pen in hand with his truck already backed up against the loading dock, the dock being the back door.

"Come on, call that assistant of yours and let's finish up. I have other business today," the veritable meat man said.

With that the meat guy opened the back of his truck, and inside, inside the freezer Krot saw that young man from before. Krot wondered why he wasn't seated in the cab with the meat guy, so he inquired with the man in the overalls as to the condition of his, Krot's counterpart's manner of transportation for today.

"I caught him eating from my loads. This is his punishment. Got it now? Now go get someone so we can finish up, if you don't he'll freeze to death and I'll have to leave him here with you, only to be forced to pick him up later again."

"Our assistant is nowhere to be found, but I'll get the Chief to help."

"That's what I thought," the meat guy said.

"But only under one condition."

"What's that?"

"That you please, please take me with you in your freezer," explained the great yanker of chains.

After exchanging their usual glances, the meat guy made his way into the morgue. And sure enough, once he got through the swinging doors, he saw the Chief sitting at the table finally having his cup of coffee. So interrupted, Zokora gave him one of those 'up your nose' kind of looks and said:

"Yes?"

"Where's your assistant, and who'll load the meat today. I sure as hell ain't goanna do it myself!?"

"Well what about your assistant? You do have one, don't you?"

"Well…, yes I do, but he's a bit chilly today. You see, Chief…"

"Rubbish, let's bring the young man in then and let him thaw for a while. You see, meat guy," Zokora said finished with his coffee and relinquishing the cup with a thump on his desk, "I won't be doing any assisting for you here today."

"You're the boss," was the meat man's only reply.

The meat guy retraced his steps back to the back, loading door of the morgue, where he saw Krot already helping his, the meat guy's, frozen assistant out of the back of the truck. And just as the meat guy was going to suggest that they go about today's business as the Chief had said, in passing, Krot only said, and he did so to both his opposite number and to the meat guy (to the latter he said it with a gaze) "Don't worry, we'll thaw you yet."

And so it was.

17.

The Lost Man

That morning, upon opening his apartment door to collect his newspaper, Ayduk's neighbor Balaban saw a ready stack of one, perhaps two (he wasn't sure of this) daily editions laying on Ayda's door mat.

Curious as to the reason for this pile-up of news next door, Balaban, in a manner old, at least as old as he was, acceded and knocked at Ayduk's door. After hearing no answer back from inside, and seeing how it was a work day, Balaban thought nothing much of it. But being, as was proven that day in the Meat Packers' Alley, a nervous Nero, he began to question the reason for this, in his mind now well present in the day, the paper pile-up. And then he remembered his own words from when he met the couple, and mumbled into his chin below the strength of voice *I knew I was missing something.* He continued rummaging through the dates of the daily editions piled up, sniffing, bent at the waist as he was, for the smell of burning meat, or perhaps of a sound sizzling on the primer of his neighbor's morning kitchen. But there was nothing to be smelled or heard, there were just those newspaper's printed dates which he proceeded to toss and turn in his hands.

So he began to trace back his steps into his own apartment, thinking to himself, *the poor man, the poor man, lost already.*

And inside his own next door, the next door from the perspective of Ayda's front door, there was waiting his old mildewed abode. In it there was his easy chair, there was his TV set, just like the one the Lagradas' had, only the TV set of Balaban wasn't constantly radiating, for he got his news the printed way, his daily news, you understand. In the aforementioned spur of suspicion, he made his way to the kitchen window from whence he and Ayduk had seen those two late-night joggers under a lit lamp post in an argument. But one thing was now unclear to him, for he was the one who chased the jagged inter-talk of those joking joggers away, and yet he later he became confused. By later, it refers to him remembering the Meat Packers' Alley and his meeting Miss Lagrada for the first time. *Perhaps that's it!?* the old man thought. It had dawned on him that he was the one hiding and running from something inside of himself, and not Ayda, for, his neighbor had indeed gotten himself a girlfriend. And then it dawned in Balaban's head, *My God whose war have I been fighting? Whose, and against whom?*

All this, it need be said was going on inside his own dwelling, his humble abode. So he got out his own paper which he had brought in with him and began going through it, wondering to himself, *God, what's the date? What day is it today? How come I haven't seen my dear friend and neighbor since he was in my apartment last?*

Balaban went through the paper like a man mad, a madman, hissing at the ads, the flyers, the pictures of flimsy-clad women denuded for circulation sake (circulation of the newspaper naturally), his brow became rilled; his eyelashes all tangled up, forcing him to rub his eyes; to spread apart his eyelids as if by using such force, attempting to get rid of the discomfort that he felt. But Balaban's discomfort wasn't physical. It was himself he was trying to come to terms with, it being how he used to pity Ayda before, and now, precisely when he was suspecting that something was wrong with his neighbor, he was the one whom he pitied, pitied by his own person.

Balaban couldn't take anymore of such a state, both of apartment and mind. In creak of his easy chair he was up on his feet, and headed toward the door to look for Ayduk. Who knows, perhaps something had gone terribly wrong; perhaps something has happened to the fellow he once called a poor, poor man.

Out he went, his wits dwelling without. He tried to retrace his steps; he did this as always by not using the elevator, which he so loathed, but the stairs. He wanted confirmation that there was still strength in those old legs of his, making their way down to the ground floor and the lobby of his building with such evident speed and substantial stamina. First he decided to go to the Meat Packers' Alley, there was something suspicious in his mind about Draga Lagrada, but he couldn't quite place what it was, perhaps she was somehow involved in his friend's disappearance.

So there he was, Balaban that is, at the end of the Alley, right where he knew the pastry shop Ayda and Draga were going to that morning was. He remembered her mentioning something about her father regarding that little family run store, or was it Ayduk who told him that later on. It's how the pathways and footsteps of the mind of a man confused work. For the above mentioned reason, Balaban went into that pastry store, once he found it, but because he bore a look of a man out of wits, he received no answer from the staff behind the counter to his query, and even if the opposite had been the case, any eventual answer he would have received he would not have understood, since the staff knew nothing about that which he searched for.

Soon Balaban exited the pastry store all bemused looking, and look he did. Both to the left of him and, on the other side, of course, to his right, and there they were – the meat packers. They were unloading into storage their daily cut of Natives, some pink, some tawny, of yellowed Chinamen, their thick black hair the only unifying factor, of brown Indian, both bony and fat, and of the rare black African, showing an almost rainbow of colors, and he thought, but of course he thought a lot of things that morning, he even thought he saw a solitary Eskimo, or it could have been an Islander, hanging on a hook inside one such storage facility, but no dear friend of his, as far as he could see, and Balaban thought to himself, *there are no pyromaniacs among Eskimos.*

Traversing the street the way he was, Balaban couldn't find the reason for the cause of his state of mind or the state of what gruesome hell was going on in this Alley. So, having no other alternative but to adhere to what was his nature, he broke out, or rather a fox like smile delineated itself on his lips and thought to himself, *Son of a gun, he must've had enough of this retched existence and gone away; just left it all behind.*

And it being that Balaban knew not Ayduk's employer, he realized that this alleyway was where his search was going to end, that he would simply have to wait it out, at least until further information surfaced, from official investigators or otherwise. And wait it out he did, gradually descending from his hyper-induced high he was on from worrying about his neighbor's whereabouts, as he stepped, one foot after another, his way through the everyday terror that surrounded him.

Along the way he had the opportunity, or, rather, he was afforded the many privileges of smells and sounds of hydraulic machinery going about its work day business, exhaust fumes and all. The corpses to be served later, or perhaps to be prepared at someone's own choice of location, be it a homestead (rented, rent controlled, rent free, or otherwise), a supermarket, or a restaurant (deli, diner, family-style, upscale, posh, or otherwise), were all hanging within his view, making his former mind retreat back in into a more steady pace of thought and sanity; each one of those thoughts going back in on Ayduk's life, and the oddly beautiful looking young woman he was with that morning. *What was her name again?* Balaban wondered.

And at his rampage's end through the Meatpackers Alley, at the very curb of the street, the washed blood draining into the gutter below, when Balaban looked down, peering, goggling his eyes into one particular stone of curb and shouted, having raised his head in a lightning-bolt of a thought:

Lagrada! He's free! Ayda Ayduk is finally free!

In fact he had been looking at the stone of curb where Ayda had introduced him to the beautiful Miss Draga Lagrada. Hence the memory comeback.

18.

The Taxidermist

There was heard the bell atop the door of his store – the infrequent business of Pavle Pechuli. But for some reason that infrequent business of his would be proven to be in great quantity of demand shortly. It would further be proven that, for some reason, during those last days of the year's Indian summer, his, Pechuli's creatures of a stuffed nature would draw a full specter, of a wide choice, of a gallery of characters.

So, the first bell chime and the first customer. Here it is and there and then it was, or more precisely there she was, with a tout bag in one, and a trolley lagging behind in the other hand, an elderly woman reeking of the swelter from outside. He knew the kind of reek, a reek of urine of a woman past the age of sixty, covered by the scent of a cheap perfume. Her tout bag didn't seem to be that weighty, not to Pechuli anyway, but he did see a nipple of a woman's breast jutting out of the side of the trolley she was pulling, her bony torso wrapped in dirty newsprint. The trolley, unlike her bag, was indeed stuffed by, what Pechuli had gathered by the breast meat, and who knows what else, maybe a femur bone for soup broth, to go with the old lady's main course of meal.

"How may I help you, madam?" Pavle, as becomes a shop owner, asked.

"Is this where they sell firs?"

"No, madam. The fir store is four doors down this street, or you could go to the..."

"Yea, yea!" and she made her way back outside.

Now, as this was going on, i.e. as the old trolley-dragging, tout-bag carrying, old woman made her way out, the bell atop the entrance needed to chime only two times more, for at the same time as the exit was made by a wayward lady-customer, a man walked in all collected looking, as if not interested in anything Pechuli's store had to offer. He was, though, of a slender build that the usual resident of that fair city. They called him and people like them Metrosexual. For Pechuli, there was a digression to be made here regarding the noun mentioned last. As he saw it, and these are only the comments of the proprietor of that store. As he saw it psychologist knew not of the term Metrosexual, it did, however know of terms such as narcissist and latent homosexual. The point he was trying to make here is that no company ever sold a lotion, volumiser, or a PH value enhancer and such to a male by calling him a narcissist or a latent homosexual, but the phrase Metrosexual held water for those folks, did it not. *But enough about marketing, i.e. Economic Propaganda*, thought Pechuli upon this man's arrival. The slender, slick-haired sauntered over to the side glass counter of the shop where Pechuli followed his lead, for indeed, as Pechuli knew well, *the customer is always right*, now, whether that particular customer is an informed one, that's, well...

"May I help you sir?" Pechuli interrupted his thought.

And just as he was about to get the usual answer of "I'm just browsing," the bell at the front door chimed twice more times, which makes it four-times so early in the morning, and a rushed rooster-looking man came rushing in, wearing pants and a shirt completely disheveled. This second man neared the front counter, the one near the electronic till of Pechuli's store. This caused a great deal of confusion, you see, Pavle didn't know whom to attend first, the party just browsing, or the man seemingly in a hurry. So Pechuli chose the second one in, who was, as Pavle approached him, tapping his fingers nervously on the top of the glass.

"How can I help you?" Pavle Pechuli asked the hurried person.

"I want, no I need salt."

"Sir, this is a taxidermist store, we don't sell salt here."

"Bull. I know what you do, and I know how taxidermy is performed."

"I don't know what to tell you, sir..." Pechuli said, about to finish a sentence.

"Then what's that?" the rooster man inquired.

"What's what?"

"That, those little grains piled up. No, no, to your right, man."

"Oh, you mean this rodent here?"

"Rodents are mammals, aren't they?" the man said as stopped taping his fingers and was now rubbing his hands together.

"Yes, yes indeed they are mammals."

"I know taxidermy. I need that salt. I came here for salt."

"But if the gentleman knows taxidermy, the gentlemen will notice that the article isn't fully crafted yet."

"I'll give you a hundred for it, as is, right now," the man said, still rubbing his hands.

"As is what, sir?"

"As is..., unfinished..., the mammal..., the salt. I'm offering you a hundred. Will you accept my bid?"

While Pechuli was contemplating, or at least trying to contemplate on the matter of how in the world did this character know about the salt and the rodent he had shown Ayda when this one first came to his store, a lady-looking, upper-browed woman walked in, and yes, the bell at the door chime twice times more, bringing the total to six times. She entered slowly, gracefully, but it was a kind of grace such women inherit from their husbands' families.

"Sold!" Pavle said to the gentlemen who had his wallet already out of his inside coat pocket.

Just as he was to run the article through the register, the article in question being unfinished which gave Pechuli some bother, the slick, slender man from the browse before approached the till where business was being conducted and asked:

"Why don't you have any lions?"

"You mean the stuffed head of a lion, sir?" Pavle said upon collecting the hundred and handing his first paying customer of the day the unfinished rodent product.

"No, not a head. I'm in the market for a full, fully stuffed lion."

"I'm sorry, sir, we don't carry lion."

"You just carry lion heads, do you?"

"No we don't carry lion heads either."

"Then why did you mention the stuffed lion head previously?"

Then there was heard a sharp 'ohm' coming from the young man's belly, up through his hard-set lips, who then adjusted his slick hairdo and made his way out, making sure that the heels of his stepping shoes were made to be heard in a resounding, loud and hard sound, quite the opposite of how he seemed – the bells to the doors ringing once again.

Not used to this kind of traffic in his store, Pavle ran the back of his hand over his forehead to check his temperature and, now alone with that high-society type looking woman, decided to endure for just a while longer, i.e. just one more customer and that would be it for the morning.

"How may I help you madam?" he could tell right away.

"I'm not noticing any hog's heads on display."

"Ah, the hogs' heads," finally something he actually had in stock, "are here on the other wall. Does madam have something particular in mind?"

"Just as long as it has big tusks," the lady said.

"I see. Well, big? Let us take a look around…"

"My husband is a very hard worker. He has a study you know? A very large study. So I wish to purchase a hog's head to have it mounted over his fireplace."

"May I recommend this one," Pechuli suggesting pointing out one of his finest boars. "You see, of such a dark coat. And I think you'll find his tusks to be, in my judgment, of an ideal size for your husband's study. You understand, if it's going to be mounted over a fire place it should be black, dark haired, that is. You do know that the color black attracts and accumulates heat the best, and winter is just around the corner. Don't you agree, madam?"

"Yes, quite. Black does attract heat. I'll purchase that one. And do have it wrapped as a gift."

"Certainly," he said quite pleased with himself as the woman had failed to even attempt to negotiate a price, which allowed old Pavle Pechuli to set it as high as he thought appropriate, given the circumstances.

Pechuli dismounted the hog's head from the wall and went into the back room, behind the hanging tassels to tend to his customer's order. When all was said and done, in other words, when the hog's head was placed in an appropriate box and wrapped in gift paper appropriate to the lady expectations, who then paid for her purchase on her husband's credit card and left with her hog to her hog, Pechuli followed her to the door, closed it behind her and turned the sign hanging on the inside of the door so that it read to anyone wishing to come in "OUT ON BREAK." He then went outside, locked the store door, and walked straight to a near-by kiosk where he was asked by a young girl, for the first time that day, the question he yearned to hear, which was:

"What do you need?"

To which Pavle Pechuli answered, "I need to start smoking. That's what I need."

19.
A Social Extravaganza

It was the evening of the opera premiere outing for the Chief and his wife. The said evening in question showed much promise, as much as the architecture of the thing, the performance was being held in, at best, so it was in the mind, body and soul of Chief Zokora's wife. Not a man with time to spare, due to his weekend work at the morgue, the Chief did however tolerate his wife's requests for an occasional outing, such as the one mentioned *ut supra*, but he did manage to keep such outings as they were – occasional.

They arrived to the point of their destination by mode of a taxi, the usual crowd had already gathered at the entrance of the thing, usual as a crowd going to see a classical piece of one of those ingested, digested, reworked and extracted through both ends works, of learned music. Not everyone could handle Handel, those were the Chief's long ago planted preferences as far as this type of music was concerned, barring all other forms of art.

Unlike his better half, Zokora met no one at the grand entrance hall of a grandly designed, thing of a building. His wife, on the other hand, did find many hands to shake, words to exchange, chuckles to express and kisses to blow, all with her gallant Chief by her side, a man in an utmost state of disinterestedness for the ones he was being introduced to; the ones he was about to listen on the stage and in the orchestra pit; and the ones partaking in the whole production of a form (outside of those schooled in music) which he found to be in all retarded.

So there he was, front row center, the Chief, that is, and his missus by his side, or, to be more accurate, Zokora was by her side, looking like a right man without any rights. And, boy, when those first cords of the overture hit his ear drums, the expression on his face told of a man at the wrong place, under wrong circumstances, but with the correct woman-fellow by whose side he was seated as designated on the ticket, now sweaty in his fingers, for it seemed to be the only interesting thing to the Chief, out of all he was being exposed to, once the performers got onto the stage.

"So it'll begin now, the singing?" Zokora whispered to his wife.

"Shh, be quiet. Yes, the overture is almost over."

Later, after the intermission, the Chief's tortured torment continued, but he did notice something being prepared outside in the grand hall of the thing. All was a flashing and a buzzing with handsome young men and women counterparts, properly attired for the premiere audience, setting up champagne flutes. There were hors d'oeuvres on the side tables, vestured in satin table cloths. And during that time, the time of the intermission, Zokora, before heading back into his, or at least he considered it under the circumstances, his torture trove, he asked his wife, "I'm not going to have to mingle, am I? There won't be any mingling, or filming, will there?" to which his better half answered negatively.

For God's sake, when will this stringy-singy sensationalism end? he asked himself during the second half. But, oh, it did end, and as was made obvious to the Zokora's, afterwards there was a cocktail party for the ones in attendance of the premier of which the Chief didn't even remember the title, the title of the opera that is. And among the inter-talk with his wife, holding on to a nice thick and heavy, crystal glass of scotch, the Chief finally spotted someone that he knew. Ayda Ayduk was there with a strange beautiful young woman. Having made his excuses to his better half, busy with a kind of gossip talk of her own with one of her girlfriends, Zokora rushed toward Ayda, the aged scotch all a churn in his glass. Once on the brink of Ayduk's and Lagrada's proximity, Zokora grabbed his underling by the shoulders.

"So, how was it?"

"How was what, Chief?"

By rigor mortis, excuse the phrase young lady, but your companion, it seems to me is still lost to the world. Your vacation, remember?"

"Ah, yes, my vacation. My apologies, Chief, it was very good. I would like you to meet Draga Lagrada."

"The young lady who came by to see you that day?" Zokora asked Ayda while shaking hands with Miss Lagrada.

"It's a pleasure, sir," Draga said in response to Zokora's, it seemed, absentminded handshake, at least that's how she had perceived it.

"Yes this is her, Chief."

With the introductions over, Zokora pulled Ayda to the side and, upon rejecting a helping of foods of fingers presented to him by a cater-waiter, the Chief said to Ayduk, "Where in rigor mortis were you today? I had to deal with the meat guy and his once frozen now, I hope, well thawed assistant on my own. I thought we had an agreement regarding your vacation, and its return."

"I know. I had matters to attend to, Chief." Ayda said taking a helping of a sautéed earlobe.

"Matters, what matters? What matters more than our work? The morgue won't run itself you know? These platters that you see before you won't fill themselves."

"Isn't that why we hired young Krot?"

"So, your thoughts are directed to the kid are they? Do you know he tried to reach you at your apartment today, where were you?"

It was at that point that Ayda Ayduk gestured to Lagrada to come to him, which she did, exceptionally attired, though barely so, by the by, and once she was there he said to her, "My boss wants to know why I didn't come in to work today. Would you like to tell him, ha?"

Draga Lagrada just looked at the Chief, then and there made aware by such a woman's look of the fact that his wife may be wondering as to his whereabouts, but instead of turning his olden head around to have a look at the spot from whence he had departed from the side of his better half, Zokora just rubbed the scruff of his neck with his hand, gesturing a never mind kind of expression on his face, said goodbye to the both of them and made his way back with the glass of scotch now fully empty in his hand.

"I'm glad I met your boss," Draga Lagrada said.

"You've met the kid too, remember. He goes by the name of Krot, though, as you might expect, it's not his real name."

"Oh, the one who showed me in when I came to see you?"

"Yes, that's the one."

Biding the remainder of the champagne in their flutes, Ayda and Draga, stood there for a few minutes more, and when he saw that she had finished her drink (his, of course, not yet done with), he suggested that they should leave by saying:

"Perhaps an evening walk?"

"Perhaps," Draga Lagrada replied.

20.
Butcher's Medley

"I want you to come and meet my father," Lagrada said to Ayduk as they were laying in bead of the morning, the first Saturday of the week of his return.

"You mean today?"

"I mean right now."

"What time is it?" Ayda asked.

"It's past nine. We've slept in."

"OK. And what's your father's name?"

"His name is Cosimo, Cosimo Lagrada."

"So it is."

They both got out of their warm Saturday morning bed in Ayda's apartment and headed for his kitchen's coffee and buttered toast with a leftover helping of a pie of some Easterner's kidneys they had the night before, before going to rest for the day of Friday.

They both sat at his wooden table, he with cheeks full of kidney, she sipping on an overly milky cup of coffee with a gratified look around her nose expressing thanks to Ayda for showing her his private freezer, the ample contents thereof, and the rich substances therein, the therein pertaining to Ayda himself, as an evident provider.

They took his Jeep, which was the make of his car, hard-topped as it was, left over from the war, still parked outside, in front of his building from the night before, with its trunk now well empty. Upon making their descent by means of the elevator, unlike Balaban, on the ground floor they came across the man himself, again, as he would always be found, checking his mail box first thing in the morning, until further, where he would one day remain hanging on some freezer wall along with the other ones just like him. Balaban saw them both, prompted to such a sight by the sound of the elevator door opening.

"Ah, there you are, Ayda! All week, I've been worried sick. I've looked all over town, including the Meat Packers' Alley for you – you never know. And a good morning to you Miss Lagrada."

But Draga Lagrada just nodded in response.

"I was on vacation. You shouldn't have worried so much, Mister Balaban. Any news in the mail, you know, any post cards from friends who might know?"

"Now. But what's there to be done about frisking postcards when you're my age. Now, I need to go to the bathroom, so if you'll excuse me..."

"Are you?..."

"No, Ayda, I'm not going to be taking the freaking elevator."

As Balaban made his way to the stairs, and having grabbed hold of the railing of the stairwell, he turned to Miss Lagrada and said, "I'm sorry, young lady, you know, I had forgotten your name while I was looking and searching for your boyfriend here. Otherwise, I would have tried to contact you."

"It happens to the best of us, Mister Balaban."

"Pasha!" Balaban uttered taking his first step on the first step of the stairway up to his old man's apartment with only an official magazine of sorts, from the Ministry, in his other hand – still no post cards, it had been a while since he had gotten his last one, which could only suggest ill news.

The Jeep started just as it had been left last night – in neutral gear. Ayda pulled up and placed down the hand brake, push-

ing on a button, and the two of them disjointed their place of me-
chanical stillness, curbing away toward Lagrada's street, toward
Cosimo's butcher store.

It was Saturday morning as yet, not near noon, so the mo-
torized traffic was scarce. It didn't take them long, the wheels and
the chassis of the car to recall and therefore adjust to the streets
leading to Miss Lagrada's building where, next-door, Cosimo's
store was already open.

"Don't park in front of the butcher's," Draga Lagrada said
as he was about to.

"Why not?"

"Just park in front of my front door. There's a vacant space
right there."

"I see it, but why?" Ayda asked, bemused.

"Because I want it to be a surprise."

"You don't wish your father to see me coming."

"No."

So she said; so he parked the Jeep; so the two of them made
their way to the right of her front door, toward the butcher's; and
so they went in. It was then that Ayda saw Cosimo, after Draga
pointed to her father, all busy in the morning business of butchery
with his customers. It was then that Ayda heard Cosimo Lagrada
shouting above the crowd assembled:

"Today we have things fresh, all of which will in your guts
mesh: loins of an old lady; athlete pâté; neighbors' cuts; a bit of a
lawyer's stiff neck; supple breasts from those who never rest, who
dance the night away, accepting every advance; cured killer's lips;
muscled thighs and soup hips; schoolboys ribs; shy liver of a gorge
giver; groin with no balls of a cop on call; shingles of a priest in
a stew you want to eat; tongue of a writer, you'll lick the plate,
buttocks fat and great; giblets of a politician to steady your nerves
before voting as he deserves; the less we speak of the intestines
the better – though the sausages are delicious; something ground

of a CEO, this one was quite the fatty, better you should eat him then to have his meat pecked by a murder of crows, on the spikes around town; lean kebabs in various sums; the dentists toothless gums; new from the banker, rich with no fat to embellish, meat of his shoulders for your interest-less relish, so that you live to see better days, some more sausages from the boss who pays you; from a salesman, door to door, or on the other end of a phone, and on sale, rosy thighs from an A Level schoolgirl for you to crave; pickled wrists of a monopolist. It's not a nifty rhyme, I know, that's how it is when hunger's for show. Whatever your heart desires, our meat is your meat to hire...

"Common, we'll go in through the back way. I really want you to meet him," Miss Lagrada said.

"Having heard what I have, I do so want to meet him to. The gentlemen strikes me as quite lyrical."

"Yes. That's my father."

21.
Leftovers

On his final out-sail on the river that evening, the third one; Ayda Ayduk took Pavle Pechuli along with him in his motorboat, the propeller churn of which had indeed started, once they set sail.

You see, Pechuli, now well in the know about, and having noticed a change in his friend for which he had hoped for when they were sitting back at that cursed café, with that unnerving ill serving and ill-mannered waiter talking thins to Pavle like "wait faster" and such.

The breakage of those ripple-like river waves was present that night too, even the fall had already begun, summer heat slipping them by. But there was as yet no winter winds, no gales from either bank of the river.

"Why have you dragged me out onto the river at this time of day?"

"I want to show you something." Ayda said.

"Something pertaining to anything specific, or do you have a clear picture in mind?"

"Not the kind of clear picture you're thinking of. And as far as to what it is pertaining, well…, that's something I discovered on my trip."

"You were on a trip? When was this? Why didn't you call for the sake of my unfinished, but sold anyway, stuffed rodent?!"

"Be quiet. You'll disturb the image."

"What image?! Is everything well with you, or what?"

"The image on the bridge. You know, the jumpers."

"So, what of it?" Pechuli was stumped.

"You were a jumper once too, remember."

Pavle lowered his head in shame of recollection, and upon doing so he noticed there were no more black, plastic body bags on the bottom of Ayda's motor boat; the hook fastened onto a metal handle with which Ayda had dragged him out from underneath his drown was missing as well. That being thus, Pechuli was in concordance which he proclaimed with the words, "You lead and I'll follow."

"It's not a matter of that at all, but... Just stick with my plan." Ayduk said.

"Oh, oh, my lifesaver has a plan! Taking trips!"

"Pavle?"

"Yes, what is it now!"

"Why are your lips all bitten up?"

The head of one Pavle Pechuli was made to be brought into a lowered position right when they were half-way to the bridge, the construction of which, the railing that is, was adorned by a youngish woman of blonde hair. At least that's what Ayda was able to conclude from such a distance under the lights of the bridge. Ayduk shared this piece of information with his friend and got out his binoculars from the bag, a hanging bag, for it to be able to hang around the shoulder, you understand, of their manufacture and purchase.

"So that's how you were doing it!? The binoculars, ha?"

"Just wait. We're more than half way there. Take a look for yourself."

And Ayda handed the binoculars to his friend who, in amazement of seeing living proof of a blond haired woman about to take an 'over the fence' leap down into the river as he had done once.

"So that's how you did it? And now, now do you get it?"

"That's not the point of this here our sail. I want to make sure of something. Give me those binoculars back, will you, Pavle."

But before attiring his upper nosed eyes, now well open in the night, a night shun upon by the lights of the bridge, Ayda turned off his propeller's churn, the engine, you understand, and so the two of them remained simply gliding toward the bridge, traversing the calm, ripply waves of the fall river.

And there it was, the bridge pylon, growing ever greater in their eyes, there was a span of steel, which now, from this perspective, looked ever more real and meaningful to both men. A realization was afoot, and at its root stood the blonde woman, now standing on the without of the railing guard for sure, it was visible even without the binoculars, again, as they did once, hanging down around Ayduk's neck. Ayda then picked up his oar, until then resting on the bottom of his motor boat, the until in question being the time he turned off his engines propeller churn, and his stroking the water's rippled waves, and so he rowed just a little bit closer beneath the pier, so as not to spook yet another potential suicide victim.

According to his own judgment, at one point Ayda stopped rowing, the activity of the oar had ceased and the object in question was relinquished back onto the bottom of the vessel of their night's sail.

It was then that Ayda noticed a familiar figure on the bridge, approaching the aforementioned potential jumper and attired his gaze with the optical instrument now well in his hands once more. And he saw her, he saw Miss Draga Lagrada talking to the blonde woman still on the outer edge of the bridge's fence.

"I knew it! It's her. It's always been her," Ayda proclaimed and remained hushed.

"Knew what? Her? Who?"

Ayduk took of his binoculars, stood for a brief moment, the boat rocking below him, all the while Pechuli sitting quietly as he was instructed to do by his friend with curious lines now depicted on his countenance. In such a condition, and it was a condition in which he was looking at the bridge in one, and at his friend as yet standing with the binoculars in his hand at the other. And it was at that precise point, the point mentioned prior to Pechuli lifting his gaze again toward and upwards to the bridge and indeed to two women in conversation, that Pavle saw the blonde woman being helped by the one Ayda had mentioned noticing back over the inner side of the bridge's railing. Then and thus wise he heard a thump, it was the binoculars dropping from Ayda's hand onto the bottom of his motor boat, and all that remained of that night was Ayda Ayduk's words spoken in a normal tone of voice:

"Che tipo di dramma!"

And before Pavle Pechuli could further inquire as to the meaning of those words, them being in a language he didn't understand, Ayda Ayduk did jump overboard, and he did dive into the river, and he did emerge victorious.

June-September.

Book Club Questions

1. Approximately, what year is this story set? Is it set in the past or the future?
2. Where does this story take place?
3. What led up to things being the way that they are?
4. What are Ayda Ayduk's feeling about the food that they eat? What are Draga's?
5. What does the taxidermist in the story represent?
6. What is important about the chestnut tree reference?
7. Why does Ayda Ayduk take a trip?
8. How would you describe the character of Krot? How is he important to the story?
9. What is the role of Ayduk's neighbour?
10. How would you describe Ayduk's and Pechuli's meeting?
11. How would you describe the relationship between Draga Lagrada and her parents?
12. What does the character of the chief medical examiner represent?

Born on the 9th of August, 1978 in Belgrade, Serbia, M. Vignjević left at the age of nine to live with his family in Moscow, USSR. There he attended a Russian grammar school along with both Yugoslavian language and Music schools from 1987 to 1990. Returning to Belgrade for high school, he began writing poetry in 1994, graduating to fiction in 2005.

After finishing high school in Belgrade, M. Vignjević studied Law at Belgrade University only to drop out after one year. Instead he enrolled at the Faculty for International Management at European University from which he graduated in 2003.

His novel Očevo mleko (Father's Milk) won the literary competition of the Belgrade publishing house *Arete*, and was a featured novle at the Belgrade Book Fair in 2017.

www.ingramcontent.com/pod-product-compliance
Lightning Source LLC
Chambersburg PA
CBHW030131260626
47156CB00008B/2896